WriteTime Anthology

ONE

Short Stories by Older Writers

First Published 2019 by Shoreham Press CIC

ISBN Number 978-1-5272-5138-0

For details on WriteTime competitions and publications write to:
WriteTime, PO Box 2206, Shoreham-by-Sea, BN43 9FU, UK

info@writetime.org   www.writetime.org

ONE

Short Stories by Older Writers

Printed and bound in Great Britain by
Gemini Print Ltd
Shoreham-by-Sea, West Sussex

Edited by Irene Reed and Susan Twell
Designed by Tim Gwyther and Arron Wakeling
Lead Reader Nadia Mitchell

Contents

Foreword

We are delighted to present the first WriteTime collection of short stories by older writers.

WriteTime is a trailblazing collaboration of writers, readers and editors aged over 60. All of the work published here came to WriteTime through our regular short story competitions. Some of our writers have been published elsewhere and for others it's the first time their words have seen the light of day in a printed collection.

We are immensely proud of all of our writers. It's a very brave thing to submit your work to the scrutiny of others. We hope that this anthology encourages more older writers to take part in this exciting venture that is WriteTime.

Like all good anthologies WriteTime ONE works like a kaleidoscope – it gives the reader a dazzling variety of form and colour. On one page we find Sally's mother, insisting that one of the Rolling Stones came to tea (Mick Jagger and Mum). Turn the pages and there's a quiet meditation by the fireside (Flames). Turn again and it's wartime Britain, little Lucy is being torn away from everything that once felt safe (Going Somewhere). But every story needs the reader to complete the picture. Now it's your turn. . .

City Walk
By Christopher Owen

There were twelve of them. They were walking about the city close to St Paul's looking out for trees. The Sweet Gum Tree, the London Plane, The Judas Tree, New Horizon Elms, Ginkos from China. Some of the trees weren't to be discovered.

"That's it, the Foxglove Tree," the leader of the group said. "No, no, it isn't. It should be there. My map tells me it should be."

The sun shining on a warm Sunday morning. Down side streets, away from tourists milling around St Paul's. One of their number, David Partiker, had volunteered to be the backstop, so as to make sure no-one got left behind or went astray.

Hidden squares of the city. Quite small. Many a surprise. The Postman's Square with the plaques commemorating those who lost their lives trying to save others. A boy drowned trying to save his little brother. So many drownings. And fires. A mother dies rushing back to her blazing house to save her children. And so it goes, plaque after plaque. Quiet heroes. Mid 1800s-1977.

"We'll have a cup of tea and so forth in the café now, shall we?"

"Off we go again. Everyone ready, no one missing?"

A man lies out on a bench under the fig tree.

"We'll not go too close," the leader of the group says.

The tiered garden tucked away by the Worshipful Guild of Barbers. The sky blue.

They find benches. They sit. Off they go again. The elderly band, ten women, two men. Always the same – women but few men.

Men dead or at home and unwilling to go out, or too poorly. Two women with walking canes. The London Wall, Friday Street, Number 1 Love Lane, Merrill Lynch, Aldermanbury, names which carry history forward. Little Britain, Aldersgate Street, St Martin's Le Grand.

Have you seen David Partiker? Where's David? David in his beige raincoat and rain hat. Stooping David.

He is supposed to be the backstop, bringing up the rear to make sure no-one goes missing.

His wife died last year. It's hit him hard, that's the general opinion. He's not one for talking about it. Pleasant enough though. They say he sleeps with his wife's nightie in the bed beside him. Where's David? Two of the women turn back to have a look for him. The others wait, standing about on the pavement in Wood Street.

"Where have those two gone?" someone asks.

They've gone to find David. They should have found him by now. A woman with red hair, not her own colour – used to be when she was younger, but no longer – goes to find the two women who have gone to find David.

"Where's she going?" some of them ask.

To find the other two who are looking for David.

"Christ," someone mutters.

The atmosphere is not improving.

"I've an appointment with my dentist this afternoon," says a woman with a headscarf and two plastic carrier bags.

Eight of the twelve walkers stand about, looking left and right, marooned in Wood Street. David turns up. He comes into sight around a corner unexpectedly. It's David. "Where've you been? We were worried."

"Have you seen the others?"

David in his beige raincoat stands there helpless.

"I went," he says, "to have a look at the display in the glassware shop in a street down there."

The question arises, should they wait now for the other two and for the woman with red hair. Should they wait?

"My wife," says David, "loved glassware."

They are standing about, blocking the pavement. Young women in short shorts with their legs on display, passing by, step around them and into the road.

An unspoken question arises: would they too do this walk one day? When they're elderly? It can't be imagined. They're so young. Old age so distant in time.

But they will. Some will. With their legs covered up, a woolly cardigan drawn to, buttoned up the front. Good walking shoes. The occasional pain in the hip. And was today's elderly walking group ever young? Oh yes and they too wore shorts. In the sixties. Not in the fifties. In the fifties, mostly, as some of them would seem to remember, it would have been skirts and the men would have been wearing ties.

The nine of the twelve, including David, wait. And here's the red-headed woman and the other two now. They're all here, what a relief.

"Don't go wandering off again like that, David." They say he visits his wife's grave every day.

"I'm trying to find the Silver Lime. It's on my map. But it doesn't seem to be here," the group leader says. "Are you with us, David?"

Physically, David is with the walking group and at the same time in his head he's with his late wife. He won't say, but he had seen her in the shop that sells glassware.

He turned to look at the display in the window and there she was. Her reflection, looking sad and bedraggled and at a loss. Then after a moment or two, he saw that it was himself that he was seeing, the reflection of himself in the shop window. He tried to see her again, but he couldn't. He had gone to find the others.

The woman with the red hair had taken the opportunity, while being absent from the group, while looking for David, of telephoning her husband at home. How was he? Not too good, he had said. She'd be home soon, she had said. She knew her husband was unwell, but from time to time she needed to get out and about.

"I'll not be very long. Just phone me on my mobile if you need to," she had said.

Here they were, all together again. At last. All reassembled, safely reunited.

"There's a café along by the station," the leader of the group said to everyone. "If you're off home, there's the station or some of you might like to have a coffee and a sandwich or something."

The woman with red hair sighed. She would have a quick cup of coffee and a sandwich and then go off to the Portrait Gallery, then home to her husband. She, along with a few others, followed the leader to the café.

Most of the walkers went home. David returned to the window of the shop selling glassware.

Turn Back the Clock
By Janet Killeen

The doorbell went at 11 o'clock that Saturday morning. I'd not long been up, reluctantly climbing out of sleep to face the night before. 11 o'clock, just as I was sorting out the kitchen, throwing out the takeaway cartons, scraping the plate and running the water, watching the brown-red mess swirl into the plughole.

The lager cans clink into the bin. Then the door bell.

I dried my hands on the tea towel. Opened the door, leaning against it. I don't have visitors so I was ready to repel all comers.

"Yes?" I couldn't see clearly. The morning light was slanting into my eyes. "Yes? What is it?"

"You won't remember me." A quiet, maybe a timid, voice.

A small man, grey sweater. Grey everything it seemed.

"No," I said, and moved to close the door. "No, sorry, I can't help you."

"Please," he said. "Please give me a minute."

I waited. He seemed to need to catch his breath and then he coughed, again and again, bowing his head in his hands and struggling to speak. I softened.

"You'd better come in," I muttered. I brought him into the sitting room with all the debris that I had never managed to sort and shift.

"You won't remember me."

"No," I said. And then I did.

It was like seeing something through a telescopic lens – twist and it looms large, twist again and it recedes. For a moment he expanded, inflated, boomed in my memory. Then he shrank back to what he was now. Shrivelled, old. But a memory of terror remained with me.

"Yes, yes. I remember you." I remembered not as my adult self, but as that terrified child who had hidden again and again – behind the settee, behind the doors, in cupboards, under the bed.

I also remember the days long ago, long before, when he came home from tours of duty and we would be jubilant, greeting him as the coach brought him safely back to us. Mum holding little Irene, and me leaping beside her. And he was huge in strength, scooping us children up in his arms, lifting Mum to embrace her. We would walk away to our home on the base and the days would be filled with excitement and happiness.

"I remember you," I said again. Remembered how a kind of poison had entered our lives when he came back from Iraq. A rage that he did not seem able to control, that roared and seared from him like a flame-thrower.

Shouting and shouting at Mum, so that we children fled and hid, and shouting at Irene if she cried. Yelling and flailing out with his hand or fist, sometimes catching Mum on the side of the head. We did not understand. No-one understood how he could turn from the familiar person we called Dad to this stranger, this monster.

He would go out at night and we huddled together with relief and Mum would settle us to sleep before he returned. I guess she prayed, if that's what she did, that he would come home calm. Though there were times when his voice woke us, it shuddered through the house and furniture crashed against the walls. Sometimes we heard Mum sobbing as she struggled upstairs. Irene would creep into my bed and we would lie silently, trembling, my arms around her.

He went away. Another tour of duty. Months of respite and fear and a secret longing that he might die. None of us dared say so.

Then he returned. A medal for outstanding courage. We watched him receive it, salute, step back, stamping with boots that seemed to shake the earth.

A period of quiet and then suddenly the horror

broke out again. Night after night of black and scarlet explosions of fury, like shells that erupted and left their shrapnel of rage and pain in us all. Sometimes he would sit silent for hours on the settee and we would creep around the house, terrified lest we disturb him. He would lash out, swear, shout.

Then, just before he was due to leave with his company, he turned on us. I cannot remember what triggered it. My mother was smashed against the wall, and Irene was hit wildly as she clung to my mother. They both slid down to the floor, leaving patches and trails of blood behind them.

I looked at this man who crammed my vision as a child, now so shrunken. His clothes hung wrinkled on him, his shoes were scuffed and dull. His face was old and tired and pale. His eyes filled with tears.

"I want to ask for your forgiveness," he said.

"I remember you," I said again.

"I've been searching for you," he said. "I want to ask for your forgiveness."

I reacted with an anger I never knew I could express. All my emotions, even grief, had been flattened. Now the anger awoke.

"Forgiveness? After what you did to us?"

I shrank away from him as he passed through the doorway.

I never heard from him again. But I think of him and his quest for my forgiveness, and my outrage and rejection. My craving for vengeance.

The Old Storyteller
By Robert Crockett

Homer sat under the olive trees during the long dog days of summer. His mood was dark, you might almost say wine dark. Like the sea that carried the men of Hellas to Troy. What a great line that was, he mused, absolute classic! Only a tosser like Hesiod could complain about it being overused. And what was that crap about the story being "about nine and a half years too long"? That, from a man whose main contribution to epic poetry was some old tosh about a girl opening a box! Seriously?

But today Homer was struggling. He had heard fellow storytellers talk about the Difficult Second Epic Syndrome but he had always thought it a bit of myth, until now. After his mega success with the Trojan thing the expectations for the sequel were high.

So far it was going well – returning war hero, vengeful

gods, one-eyed monster, sexy Sirens. *What's not to like?* he thought to himself. *To be honest though it did lack a real ball-grabbing ending.*

When he returned to his white-walled farmhouse, his faithful hound by his side, his wife looked up from her spinning wheel and noted her husband's subdued manner. "Not going well dear?" she said. "It's that ending isn't it?"

For someone lacking any formal education, his wife could be perceptive. As Homer often thought, a woman sitting spinning all day must think about issues other than How to Be Obedient. He considered himself quite forward-thinking on such matters.

"All your stories seem to be about men fighting, it's all sex and violence," she continued. "How about a woman outwitting a group of men for a change? Make it more realistic."

"Oh I don't know about that," Homer replied. He didn't mind a bit of controversy. That thing between Achilles and Patroclus had caused a bit of stir. It had gone down well in Athens – but then, it would. A woman outwitting men though? Was the world ready for that?

At this point, Homer's dog got up from his place by his master's side and urinated on the spinning wheel.

"Look at what that filthy old thing has done now!" shrieked Homer's wife. I was making that tunic for

Penelope. I know, I can't stand the woman, but she's got an unmarried son who would be perfect for our eldest. Too many suitors have been put off by all that wailing and doom-mongering she does. I don't know where she gets that from do you?

"Now I'll have to unpick the damn thing and start all over again."

Homer felt a thunderbolt had struck him. He looked down at his dog and for the briefest of moments, he thought he saw the image of the muse Calliope reflected in the hound's eyes.

"Argos," he said, "you're a legend. At least you will be when I've finished this sodding Odyssey."

Winter
By Lynn Loader

This particular teatime, in that unsettling hiatus between Christmas and New Year, half of her family were bickering happily over Monopoly in the conservatory. The living-room contingent were sliding into a comatose state in front of a TV repeat. The fact that it was a repeat didn't matter, they had not been able to stay awake through the first showing either.

The thing about clichés, she pondered, was they are true. Hands reached out mechanically for chocolates, shovelling them down throats lubricated with alcohol and pitching them into stomachs bewildered by seasonal excess and ill-considered food combinations.

Banking on the fair bet that each branch of her loved ones would assume that the other was taking a turn at her bedside, she closed the kitchen door and stood in the darkened hall breathing deeply, or as deeply as she could now manage. Right now she needed to escape and be nurtured by the outdoors.

Glancing up at the stained glass sunburst panel at the top of the front door, she tried to gauge the temperature outside by the quality of the light filtering in. Bleak, she guessed. *In the bleak midwinter.* Possibly also a *frosty wind making moan.* She thought back to her childhood of socks lovingly put to warm on the radiator, her mother wrapping a hairy scarf around her neck before she left for school. Her friends had mothers with Proper Jobs. Hers made jam and spooned it into jam tarts and fed them to those friends and they lapped up the mothering.

She bundled herself into a fleece over her new Christmas jumper. Christmas, even this year when time was so short, always meant a fanciful jumper, and suddenly she recalled that other constant of her childhood Christmases, the jigsaw puzzles. The series with the African wildlife was what she remembered most vividly, with those baobab trees so flat on the top and the antelopes so amazingly springy. And always so much sky. Do the edges first, and never look at the picture on the box, was her iron rule. That way it emerged slowly into focus, like unwrapping a complex parcel.

On with the gloves so thick that her hands looked like the kind children draw, with huge banana fingers, and finally out of the door. After so many days of enforced captivity, first in hospital and then convalescing at home after the surgery, she revelled in being out of doors. The glittering shock of the ice crystals made her feel slightly drunk. The air was almost too cold for her poor ravaged lungs to breathe but she gulped it hungrily anyway, everything now was a treat and a gift, not to be squandered or taken for granted.

Soon she came to the end of the paved road and her feet carried her confidently towards the path into the wood. She had slipped a torch into her pocket, another Christmas tradition, each year's bigger or brighter or more cunningly designed than the last. This one boasted so many lumens that it was apparently visible from space. She did not need it to find her way. Somehow she felt sensible and well prepared by having it with her.

Her boots led her along the familiar track up the slope towards the fallen log where she had rested on so many mornings, listening to the birdsong and catching the occasional glimpse of deer drinking at the stream. The trees were bare now, but her mind's eye coated them extravagantly in the sharp green of the coming spring.

Since the diagnosis, everything had become precious and luminous. She was trying not to miss a single moment. They had said a year if she were lucky. That meant one more seasonal cycle. She had already used up the summer and the autumn. Now the winter was running through her fingers and soon the spring would be all she had. She had made her peace with this fact, indeed, given the choice, she would have wished for spring in Yorkshire to be her last impression of the world she had to leave. She sat down on her log, panting from the unaccustomed exertion.

An owl hooted precisely like a cliché of an owl in a dark December wood. It was answered by another. She peered up but could see nothing. She had never once managed to see these owls but still she went through the ritual of craning her neck and squinting against the starry sky. The paired-up birds were part of her personal landscape.

She got back up and made her way along the stream now frozen in parts while other sections gushed busily. How did that work, she wondered. The list of things she had to accept she would never know was growing longer by the day. Still the stubborn habit of asking questions had not deserted her. It was a quiet form of revenge against the dying of the light.

Upwards now to the skyline, past the warren and the logs curving like arms hugging the charred patch where generations of people had made their camp fires. She turned off along the track which in the late spring would saunter through the bluebell patch. She smiled to remember the first time she had come upon that wash of blue, so subtle that you could not see one individual flower if you looked straight at it. It was visible only out of the corner of your eye. She recalled a TV astronomer explaining that the best way to see certain faint stars was to look away and try to catch them in your peripheral field of vision.

The bluebells had given her a surge of joy and for years she had gone back every day for as long as they lasted. The knowledge that they would come again – that even now, deep beneath the icy grip of winter, renewed life was lying latent – gave her comfort.

She turned right and struggled up the slope. The fence lay tumbled here, but she always entered the field through the rusty gate she loved. It stood in isolation between its posts, not attached to anything on either side, with a slightly surreal gravity that never failed to appeal to her. Slowly downhill now, past the heronry in the big clump of trees. On the edge of the moor she could just make out the huddled bouldery shapes of the sheep. It would not be too long now before they would have their new lambs.

And then the final stretch down the grass-grown and long-abandoned paved road towards the lake. Her lake, as she always thought of it, caught like a shard of mirror. Her shaky torch beam wavered out across the frozen expanse, illuminating gulls and a pair of moorhens in the reeds. She could remember the time before the lake, when it was just an artist's impression in a promotional brochure for the housing development. It had been called into being by men and embraced quickly by nature. The moorhens were the first. She had never seen a moorhen fly but somehow they had found this new lake and bird-word had spread.

The old pang of superstition jabbed. Had it been tempting fate to move into a house built on the site of an old TB sanatorium? Who could say? Would she have fallen ill wherever they had moved to?

She would like to be there when the lapwings hatched out. By even thinking about the coming spring, was she somehow subtly jeopardising her chances of making it that far? The thought was like a splinter in her struggling brain.

The lake lay still and bright. It calmed her turbulent thoughts. The frozen mud at its edges bore merely a glitter of frost where the footprints of the birds could still be seen preserved as if under glass in a museum. The tale they told of life going on without her was obscurely cheering. Smiling gently, and gasping to catch her breath, she brushed the thin layer of crystals off the splintery wooden bench at the water's edge and lowered herself heavily, wincing as the cold penetrated through all her many layers of clothing and encountered her feverish skin. Perhaps she would just take a little rest and try to slow down her breathing and tame her pounding heart.

So quiet and peaceful. Her mind began to empty. The snow began to fall gently.

As You Sow
By Jim McGuirk

George forced down the last of his cornflakes and lit a cigarette. A few drags later his hands were shaking a lot less.

He put his breakfast dishes in the sink and made his way to the kitchen door. As he reached for the handle a surge of fear swept over him. Peering out into his back garden he could just make out the end of the greenhouse from behind the hedge.

That had been Ethel's idea. "Why not grow a dividing hedge?" she had barked. "Then we could grow all the vegetables down there by the greenhouse, and all the flowers up here by the house."

George remembered how pleased she had been with her idea. She kept having these ideas and he kept having to implement them.

He ventured into the garden and followed the curves

of the crazy-paving path down to the greenhouse. George normally got so much pleasure from the flowers and plants along the way. Today he was oblivious to the scents and colours they offered him in greeting.

His mind jumped back to last year's show at Croxteth Hall and its terrible aftermath.

They had been carefully nurturing their prize marrows ready for the gardening show last August Bank Holiday. One of Ethel's was particularly large and beautifully formed. One of George's was also beautifully formed – and it was a foot longer than Ethel's.

George had stolen the march on Ethel. While she was doing all the shopping and housework, George had been up at 6am every morning, talking, singing and playing recorded music to his prize marrow – a trick he had learned from an old gardening friend.

He was in no doubt his beloved plant would win the competition. His confidence was shattered, however, when Ethel came in from the greenhouse shedding a monsoon of tears.

"I fell over in the greenhouse, George," she sobbed, her eyes swivelling under the tears as she tried to gauge his reaction.

He put his arms around her and patted her. "Never mind, sweetheart," he said, oozing sympathy. "What's this all over your dress?"

She screwed her eyes up tighter and squeezed out a few more tears. "I'm terribly sorry, George, I fell on one of your marrows and squashed it as flat as a pancake."

The sobs grew louder in anticipation and George felt as though someone was tying his intestines like bootlaces.

"Which one?"

Ethel sobbed even louder. George wondered if he was imagining it, but there seemed to be a hint of laughter mixed in with the sobbing.

"The biggest one," she wailed.

After that it had been all-out war. George started getting out into the greenhouse at 5am. He gave his remaining marrows the best of everything. With two weeks to go to the show, one of them started to grow at a fantastic rate and was catching up with Ethel's.

George played music to it, sang and recited poetry to it. He even danced Sammy Davis's Mr Bojangles routine to entertain it. One evening, just before he came into the house, Ethel caught him kissing it goodnight.

Show day arrived. It seemed that both George's and Ethel's marrows were the same size and equally unflawed. It was up to the judges to decide.

Driving home after the show, George maintained a stony silence, his face like thunder. Ethel had sat in the passenger seat cooing and polishing her silver cup with her sleeve. And later they were down by the potato patch when she mocked him again about flattening his marrow. That was when he snapped.

He had been surprised at how easily his favourite spade had cut off Ethel's head, legs and arms. Within minutes, Ethel's body had been reduced to a mass of red and white pulp. The head and hip bones went straight into the rubbish bin.

George felt strangely remote and unemotional as he mixed Ethel with the compost. Her blood would be good for the tomatoes, he told himself.

Now George was nearly at the greenhouse. He made a determined effort to regain control of his nerves. He pressed his face against the glass and looked inside. He jumped back in sheer terror. He hadn't imagined it. The tomatoes were still there.

Overcome by a mixture of denial and macabre curiosity, George stepped inside the greenhouse. He approached the plants. They were unusually large and well-developed for the time of the year. The fruits were sturdy and fully ripened.

Every tomato was an exact replica of Ethel's face. Each one was shouting in a high-pitched, squeaky voice. Each one straining to be heard. Each one judging and insulting, chipping away at George's remaining sanity. Suddenly, as the tomato plants entwined their vines around his limbs, they spoke in unison.

"I knew you'd come back to me George," they said. A large thick vine tightened around his neck. "Now we'll be together forever."

Second Home
By Terry Parsons

"Remind you of anywhere?" a jubilant Chief Navigator asked the Captain, turning away from the main telescope.

The ship's long-range scanners had confirmed that this new planet contained a great deal of water and its atmosphere had a high oxygen content. Closer in it presented a reassuringly blue appearance.

"It certainly looks promising. . ."

"Highly promising! They'll be thrilled back at Base. Have you sent off a message yet?"

"No, and I shan't until we've conducted a thorough investigation. I don't want to get their hopes up again, only to find that there's something – some impediment we can't even imagine – that would make colonisation unviable."

And so, with the mother ship keeping well clear of the planet, a scouting team set off in a small reconnaissance craft. The Captain impressed upon them that theirs was purely a fact-finding mission.

"Should this planet contain any intelligent beings you will not, at this stage, make contact with them. Nor will you risk being detected. You may land if you consider it safe, but light-deflecting equipment will be operational at all times to ensure invisibility."

When the team returned the Captain assembled the entire crew to hear their report-back.

The geologist spoke first. "A somewhat younger planet than our own, I should say. Craggier – erosion having had less time to do its work, but of course that's no bad thing. Various familiar rock formations – shale, sandstone, sedimentary, volcanic. We did detect a few active volcanoes, but not as many as might be expected on a comparatively young planet. Shouldn't pose any serious problems."

"So far so good then," said the Captain. "Let's keep things in evolutionary order, shall we?" He turned to the biologist. "What about vegetation?"

"Firstly, I am delighted to report that, on landing, yes of course we did land, we found we had no need for any supplementary respiratory equipment or filters – we could breathe the atmosphere!" the biologist told the assembled crew.

A huge cheer went up.

"Now take a look at this," he said, pointing his image-gatherer at the wall-screen and beaming onto it pictures of grasses, shrubs and trees. "Can you believe it? Deciduous and evergreen! As you can see, some of these leaves are beginning to turn brown. This planet, too, has an inclined axis – it has seasons!" Another cheer.

"And now some flowers. . . Aren't these beautiful? But look closely and you'll see that they, like ours, are not without their thorns!"

There were murmurs of delight from the crew. Someone said, "If ever a planet looked ripe for colonisation. . ."

"Let's not get carried away," interposed the Captain gently. "We've yet to hear about animal life. I'm assuming there is some?"

"Oh yes, lots of animal life." The zoologist now took centre stage.

"First, the good news. Again, much of it not so very different from what we have back home. Insects. . ." Images of small creatures now occupied the screen, some flying, others crawling.

"Reptilian. . . what you see here could be one of our own sand lizards. A huge variety of birds. Fish in the oceans and streams – not so very different from our own fish. Creatures that have evolved in water are likely to share at least some characteristics – scales, fins. . . Any deep-sea creatures were, of course, way beyond our powers of investigation but I'd be surprised if there aren't some. Who knows? Perhaps there are giant octopuses with vast numbers of tentacles, perhaps there are."

The Captain raised a hand. "I think you are rather toying with us, Professor. You know what we are all most anxious to hear about – mammalians, creatures with fur, hair. . ."

"Oh yes, no shortage of them, either. Rodent-like animals. . ."

More images were thrown onto the screen. "Big horned beasts of bovine appearance. . . And these cute little furry creatures very like our own felines. What you see here is a litter of one of the smaller varieties."

Cries of endearment came from the assembled crew. "Oh aren't they sweet!"

"What little darlings!"

"A planet with pets provided!"

"And these rather strange tree-dwelling animals," continued the zoologist. "Queer little brutes, aren't they? But harmless enough I think. As you see, not much like anything we've got at home. But on a planet so distant from our own it would be amazing to find some near equivalent of every life form. . ."

"Sounds almost too good to be true," remarked the Captain. "And perhaps it is. You started off by saying, 'First, the good news' – that rather implied that there was going to be some bad news too."

"I'm afraid there is." The zoologist's voice took on a sombre tone. "We now come to what I suppose I have to call this planet's most successful or, rather, dominant creature. It's the one truly alien life form that we found."

"How disappointing," said the Chief Navigator. "I was half expecting that you were going to reveal that the planet's most dominant creature was perhaps at an earlier stage in evolution but something like ourselves."

"No such luck. These creatures – I'll show you some pictures in a moment – are nothing like us. By no means devoid of intelligence, they construct buildings. They have machines, crude by our own standards, of course.

"Your prohibition with regard to making contact, Captain, proved to be quite unnecessary! They are capable of remarkable savagery. We saw various regions of conflict, probably fights for territory, but unfortunately not enough."

"Why do you say 'not enough'?" the Captain asked.

"Because, apart that is from themselves, these creatures seem to have no natural predator. Consequently they have spread over most of their planet in vast numbers. At a rough estimate I should say that there must be billions of them, several billion too many. Huge tracts of land have been made over to accommodate them, at what expense to plant and other animal life we can only guess, but it's certain to have been pretty devastating."

"Are you saying that they are doing to their planet what we were once in danger of doing to ours?"

"I am saying just that. And if there is to be any colonisation, any at all, then there will need to be a vigorous cull to contain these prolific creatures."

"I think," said the Captain, "that it's about time we had a look at them. Sounds as though we might be in for a shock."

"Judge for yourselves. Here we have a male, a female and a couple of their offspring."

Gasps of surprise, but by no means revulsion, went up from the crew. "Well, at least they're not green!" someone said.

"Why green should ever have been the colour associated with aliens, I have never understood," said the zoologist testily.

"A cull does seem a bit drastic," mused the Chief Navigator. "They don't seem so bad after the initial shock. The little ones do have a certain appeal. . . There are some who rather like exotic pets."

"I'm not suggesting that they be wiped out, of course I'm not, that would be an outrage to scientific research. But colonisation or no colonisation I still say there ought to be a cull. Why allow these heedless, quarrelsome creatures to destroy a perfectly good planet?"

"Those creatures you showed us just now – the ones you couldn't compare with any of our own species – they seem to have some similarities with what we're looking at here," the Captain said. "Could these have evolved from them, or something like them?"

"Possibly. But that has no bearing on the necessity of a cull."

"I'll need to think about that. . . Maybe I should take a trip there myself."

"Why not? But I am sure, Captain, that you will come to the same conclusion. After all, they are only animals. Look at them – just two arms and only the one head."

Such Stuff as Dreams Are Made of
By Janet Hender

She awakes from the dream feeling tense and edgy. It is the only dream she seems to have or at least the only one she remembers. She calls it her anxiety dream, not exactly a nightmare but certainly unsettling and it follows a familiar pattern.

She finds herself in a strange town. Emerging from a municipal-type building she struggles to remember in which direction the car park lies. The routes to several are indicated by nearby signs. Which one had she chosen? She curses herself for not taking more careful note when she arrived. In a state of increasing panic, she goes on to search first one and then another looking for her little car.

What should she do? Has it been stolen or has she merely failed to spot it? Was there yet another car park she has neglected to check? Would the police be able to help her? Probably not, she thinks. It is now growing dark.

She wakes up.

For a moment anxiety lingers but then she picks out the reassuring shapes of the bedroom furniture in the growing light and moves her hand to feel the emptyspace beside her. She used to tell him when she'd had the dream and he would chuckle a little in a sympathetic way and tell her she'd better stop eating cheese at night.

She would go to see him later and tell him about it even though he doesn't know her now.

Falling into the Dark
By Linda Roberts

Isla screamed out in pain. She lay transfixed by the sound of her echo in the darkness. Then silence. She let out little sobs between rasping breaths. The pain, all the way down her right leg, her elbows, her shoulder. Her head throbbed. She could taste blood. Was it her lip, her tongue? Had she knocked out a tooth? Or even worse, was she coughing it up?

She had no idea how long she'd been lying there. She listened hard, but the only sound she could hear was her own breathing.

She was lying almost flat, propped up by what felt like a pile of shingle or stones. Her eyes were slowly becoming accustomed to the darkness and she could see that whatever was in front of her had a slight sheen to the surface. Was this a rock face? Isla tried to piece together the events that led up to where she was now.

Had it been minutes, or was it hours?

She'd been walking through Netherton woods with Mitzi, her little wire-haired terrier. Where was Mitzi? She called out, "Mitzi, Mitzi, where are you girl?" No response.

She remembered having thrown a stick for her to fetch, and then hearing a distant rumbling noise followed by a loud whoosh and the ground beneath her feet literally opening up. Before she had time to do anything, she'd slipped into an ever-widening cavern. She recalled that she seemed to have been falling forever. How long she had been lying there she couldn't tell. She felt in her pocket for her phone. "Ouch! Oh, my God. Oh, my God!" she screamed.

She wrestled her phone out of the pocket at last, every movement causing her to wince with pain. The screen was cracked in places, but she managed to see the time, 4.09. "That means I must've been down here for about forty minutes," she said, with a sob leaking out of her throat. "I left the house just before three." Again trying to recall her movements up to this point. "I must've knocked myself out for a while."

Gingerly she touched the side of her head which was still throbbing, there was a large bump starting to form and her fingers felt sticky. Blood? She felt sick.

"Pull yourself together, Isla. Take some deep breaths," she told herself.

She remembered walking across the field to the woods. It had been raining and Mitzi had jumped into puddles and buried herself under the piles of wet and rotting leaves.

Again she called out for the little dog. But the only sound was the echo reverberating back on itself. Isla hoped that Mitzi had managed to get back home and someone would realise she was on her own. "Please God, let that be the case. Please let her bring someone to find me."

She continued to work out what exactly she'd fallen into. Was it an old mineshaft? Coal mining had gone on in this area many years ago, the pits had been closed down and the shafts filled in, supposedly. But what she could feel around her didn't feel like coal.

It was cold now. She began to shiver. The pain was getting worse, but at least she could no longer taste the blood. She managed to look up and above her head she could just see a pinprick of light.

Isla called out again until her throat was hoarse. Her voice echoed in the darkness, the sounds getting quieter and quieter. She had to be somewhere where a sound could travel, somewhere like a tunnel. She reached out her left hand to try and feel her surroundings. Her fingers traced the surface, there were definite lines – it was brickwork. A wall of bricks. What was this? In a flash she remembered the old railway tunnel. She'd heard of it from local people over the years. Apparently the kids from school used to go down to the 'tunny' to smoke or drink or generally hang out. The railway line and the tunnel had been closed down for decades. What had been the entrance had become overgrown with weeds and brambles.

She reached out her left leg and her foot hit something as hard as rock. She moved her foot across what she'd found, it was straight, yes, that had to be the iron track, how lucky was she not to have hit that during her fall.

She looked up again. Was it her imagination or was that pinprick of light less bright now? Was that a drop of water she could feel on her face? Was it raining?

She tried her phone, obviously no signal, but was the torchlight still working? She'd forgotten about that. Relief, the light still worked.

It soon occurred to her that the sheen she could see on the brickwork was moisture and she could see water trickling down the wall. Shining the light on the ground she could see puddles lying amongst the ballast and then she heard a splash. Then another, followed by scratching noises. She was no longer alone in the tunnel. The sounds were getting closer, she let out a scream and the scurrying vermin quickly ran away, but not before she felt one of them jump on her foot. She attempted to kick it away, which brought another sharp stabbing pain to her injured limb that ran all the way up her leg.

How long would it be before the rats came back?

Isla tried to shift her position and sit up. She placed her hands either side of her hips and pushed with all her might. "Ignore the pain, ignore the pain," she reminded herself. But this time her hands had sunk into wet mud and she could feel her bottom sinking too.

The panic started to rise in her once more. Her feet felt wet. Although her right leg was now quite numb with the cold and the pain, she was sure her legs were getting wetter.

Water was coming in from somewhere, but where? Was it rainwater? An underground stream perhaps? Or something else?

Then a dreadful thought struck her. Supposing some underground water pipes from the old railway had become dislodged by the cavern opening up? The sound of water trickling was becoming louder, but it was no longer a trickle.

Isla heard the distant sound of a dog barking. Was that Mitzi? She'd come back to find her? Relief coursed through her aching body. She tried hard to focus on the barking noise. But the sound coming from the depths of the tunnel was drowning it out. Then the cold, filthy water struck her face.

Mick Jagger and Mum
By Mary Charnley

"I had tea with Mick Jagger yesterday."

"Did you Mother? That was nice. What did he have to say?"

"Well you know, we just sort of chatted about the old days. He's getting a bit old though. He dyes his hair."

"How do you know?"

"Well it's gone a bit white at the roots and some of his teeth are missing. He smells a bit too, like old wee."

"Oh, Mum. Have you been dreaming again? It was Prince Charles the night before. You said he dropped in for a glass of sherry."

"Oh, no, that was just a dream. I'm glad that one wasn't true. I can't stand him and that Camilla woman." Sally kissed her mum on the cheek.

"He did, you know."

"Did what?"

"He did come to tea. He liked my scones. I gave him a pot of that strawberry jam I made. He's a very nice man really."

"Are you going to have a cuppa Mum?"

"Ooh, yes please. Not one of those fancy things, proper tea. He likes proper tea he said, you know, builders' he called it. Two sugars and not too much milk."

"Who? Who does?"

"Mick of course. Haven't you been listening to a word I said?"

The house smelt a little, of cooking and dust and talcum powder and something else. What was it? The smell of old age? No, something different, a sweet sharp smell. It reminded Sally of her youth, late nights at Uni, sharing a spliff. No, surely not.

"Mother? Have you been smoking again?"

"Me? No, of course not. It was Mick, he asked if I would mind, offered to share it but I said no. I can tell you I was tempted though. No, I had a nice cup of tea instead."

Her mother put down her cup and started singing, in her thin asthmatic voice:

I can't get no satisfaction,
I can't get no. . . oo chain reaction
But I try, but I try. . .

Sally looked around the room, plumped up cushions

on the sofa, went over to her father's old chair.

"Leave it! I don't want you touching that. No one's allowed to touch that chair, ever again."

"But Mother... This place could do with a good clean..."

"Well never mind that, you're not touching that chair."

"Why ever not?

"Cos that's where he sat, you know, Mick Jagger. I can see his imprint on the cushion."

"Oh, don't be so ridiculous Mum. It was only a dream."

"Well you can believe what you like. I tell you he was here, yesterday afternoon, drinking tea and eating scones with strawberry jam."

"Have you had any lunch?"

"No, Mick's taking me out to dinner."

Sally sighed.

"I've still got all his records you know."

"What records, you threw loads of stuff away when you moved here."

"But I wouldn't have got rid of those. No, they were special. I was telling Mick all about my collection. He said he'd bring me the new CD. They're still doing concerts you know. Amazing, and that Keith whatsisname. He's still alive and all. You wouldn't believe it would you, all those drugs. Mick says his wife's had another baby and asked him to be godfather. Not much godly about him though."

"Are you taking your tablets Mum? You know how you get if you don't take them."

"Mick's going to call round this evening, about six o'clock."

"What?"

"I said, Mick's going to call round later, take me out to dinner. Are you deaf or something?"

"I heard what you said. You've got to stop this nonsense. It was only a dream."

"It wasn't. He sat there, look, you can see his imprint on the cushion." Sally went over, saw nothing, only a few cat hairs.

"Would you mind having a look in the garage, dear?"

"What for?"

"The record player and the records of course. Dad put them there the other day, said they were taking up too much space."

"Mum. . . Dad's been dead for five years. I'm sure we took them to a car boot sale. You asked me to, said you didn't want them around anymore, reminding you of him."

"I'll go myself then," she said, "if you can't be bothered." She hobbled out of the sitting room on her two sticks, and through the kitchen to the garage.

She returned, struggling with a cardboard box and laid it triumphantly on the table.

"Here you are," she said. "I told you so."

Sally looked at her watch. Did she need to leave? Perhaps she could spend a little time with her mother, play let's pretend. She'd read somewhere that that's what you should do with dementia. Try to live in their world a little, don't keep telling them they're wrong.

Her mother was slowly making her way up the stairs.

"Where are you going?"

"Getting changed, he'll be here soon. I thought I'd wear that dress I always wear at Christmas, and those pearls your Dad gave me when we got married."

"Come back down, Mum. Let's have look in the box shall we?"

Sally opened the box. Inside there were LPs, lots of them *Rolling Stones Live*, *Out of Our Heads*, *Emotional Rescue*. Young faces staring out from bright covers. A large picture of Mick Jagger signed on the back, *To Shirley from Mick, August 1964*. Old tickets from live performances all over the country. She'd never known her mother had been such a fan.

How sad it is, how I never talked to her about her youth.

She put the box down and went upstairs. Her mother was struggling with her dress.

"Come here Mum, you've got it on back to front."

She pulled the dress over the old lady's head, kissed

her gently on the neck where the skin was still soft and white.

"You can't go out to dinner with your dress on back to front. What would Mick think? Now what shoes are you going to wear?"

She saw that her mother's nails needed cutting. They were yellow, starting to curl inwards. She made a mental note to call the chiropodist. So many things to remember. She glanced at the picture by her mother's bed. Her and Dad, the day they got married. Her mother had been so beautiful. *Why did I never see it before?*

Sally picked up the pearls and fastened them around her mother's neck.

"There," she said, "all ready? Now how about spending a penny before you go."

She was on her way downstairs when there was a knock at the door. An old man stood on the step, dishevelled, and in need of a shave. She noticed the egg stains on his tweed jacket. He smiled at her and held out his hand.

"Mick," he said, "Mick Jagger. Pleased to meet you."

She recognised him then, the old boy from the Day Centre. Last week he'd been Frank Sinatra.

She helped her mother down the stairs, holding her hand and feeling the lumpy bones, the swollen knuckles. Such a feeling of tenderness came over her.

Would it do any harm. Two lonely old people?

She turned to leave, the beat of music heavy on the air. Sticks thrown aside, they were dancing.

Parallel Lives
By David Watson

Lucy sat precariously on the cliff, staring down at the water below. The sun was hot on her back and she was tempted to dive into the sea. The water did not look inviting though, no Mediterranean blue here, more a murky brown, with flecks of foam on each wave.

She didn't know how it happened – it was as though the ground moved but she found herself tumbling down to the sea below. She landed head first into the icy cold water and fell further and further into its depths.

The landing had forced the air out of her lungs and it was quickly being replaced by the foul-tasting water.

Then her fall abated and she could see the sunlight above. She slowly began to rise towards it. She broke the surface and once more felt the sun's heat. She spluttered and gasped as she tried to empty the water from her lungs but she began to drop below the surface again.

This time she closed her mouth tightly and stretched herself upwards once more. As she broke the surface for a second time, she turned onto her back. She'd heard what happens if you go down for a third time.

As she lay floating on her back Lucy thought it was odd that the sun felt so hot but the water so cold. Paddling around in a circle she looked for anyone who could help. She could no longer see the land, just endless waves.

She was scared but her natural survival tendencies began to kick in. The sun was low to her right, which must be west, so land should be in that direction. She flipped over and began to swim – more a doggy paddle really, but she was determined and now had a goal.

Lucy had no idea how long she had been in the water and although she would never admit to it, she was close to the limit of her endurance. But at that moment she saw a cliff in the distance.

Re-invigorated she raised the effort to swim towards the cliff. However in that moment of hope her joy was crushed. The cliff seemed so high, no inlet, no beach, just endless cliff.

In despair she flipped onto her back once more and stared up into the sky. The sky, as if from nowhere, clouded over and the waves began to smash her against the cliff-face violently.

Outside the Lord Nelson pub overlooking the North

Sea, Dave and his mate John were enjoying a cool beer in the sunshine.

John's hand rested on Dave's arm as he raised his glass, "Wait a minute Dave, there's something in your beer."

Dave stared down into his pint glass.

"It's a ladybird." He dipped his forefinger into the glass then raised it with a flick into the air.

Lucy found herself tumbling through the air.

She instinctively unfolded her wings and began to fly towards the warmth of the sun.

The Dim Reaper
By John Maskey

It had been a fantastic party. The booze flowed, the music was great and I had started to make my move on a dark-haired girl who had been smiling at me.

Then everything went black.

The music stopped, the drink in my hand disappeared and there was no one to be seen.

Suddenly a towering figure in a full-length robe emerged in front of me. There was no face, just two red orbs like burning coals staring from inside the hood.

A skeletal hand clutched a scythe as tall as he was.

"I am Death!" boomed a voice.

I can't remember how much I'd had to drink but I sobered up in an instant. It took a lot of willpower not to wet myself.

"I am Death!" he roared again.

"What, er, what do you want from me?" I stammered.

"I can't be dead. There's nothing wrong with me."

"You, Arthur Barrington!" A bony finger poked out of his sleeve into my face. "The time you have been allotted is at an end. You will follow me and I shall escort you from this vale of tears."

"Where to? I don't want to go anywhere. I want to stay here. I, er, wait, hang on a second. What did you call me?"

"I called you by your name, Arthur Barrington! Your seventy three years on this earthly plane are at an end. I command you to come with me now!"

"Wait a minute," I protested. "That's not my name."

"What?"

"It's not my name. Well, it is and it isn't. You called me Arthur Barrington but I'm Barrington Arthur. My surname is Arthur and my first name is Barrington, although everyone calls me Barry."

There was a pause.

"Oh bugger," he muttered.

"You also said I was seventy three years old. I'm thirty seven."

"Are you sure?" said Death raising his voice again.

"Of course I'm sure! Do I look seventy three?"

The hooded figure leaned in for a closer look.

"Not really, but it's a bit dark in here."

"Look, can you just talk normally instead of sounding all melodramatic, like some ham actor."

He raised the scythe in the air with his bony hand and brought down the shaft with a deafening bang. I covered my ears. My body shook.

"I am Death!" he thundered. "I have been the most terrifying image in human culture for centuries. I can hardly turn up sounding like David Beckham."

"Okay, fair enough. But could you just knock the volume down a bit? Look, it's obvious you've got the wrong bloke. Close, but wrong. So could you just send me back to the party? You see, there was this girl I liked the look of and I. . ."

"I'm sorry, I can't," he said, his voice suddenly quiet.

"What's that supposed to mean?" It was my turn to shout.

"You're dead. Sorry."

"Dead? How can I be dead when I'm talking to you?"

"I'm afraid that just by looking at me brings about your death."

"You can't do this to me. You are the one who messed it up." I jabbed my finger at him. "You've got the wrong man and you know it."

"I've said I'm sorry. What more do you want?"

"I want my life back, that's what. I'm only halfway through my three score years and ten. I'm going to Tenerife at the end of the month. And there's that girl at the party. I don't see why I should be dead when it's not my fault. This is your mistake and you owe it to me to put it right."

"I suppose so. I'll see what I can do," sighed Death. He passed me the scythe. "Here, hold this while I call the office."

His hand let go of it too early and the blade swung round dangerously. If I hadn't ducked it would have taken my head off.

"Watch what you're doing!" I shouted. "You nearly killed me a second time."

"Oh, don't worry about that. The blade's plastic."

"Plastic?"

"Yeah. Health and safety."

From the sleeve of his robe he pulled out a mobile phone and punched in a number, his skeletal fingers clacking on the plastic. He turned away and talked quietly so I couldn't hear what was being said.

Then he turned towards me holding the mobile away from him.

"Are we in Newcastle?"

"Yes," I said. "Newcastle under Lyme."

"Not Newcastle upon Tyne?"

"No."

He turned back to the phone. There were mutterings I couldn't make out before he finally ended the call.

"Let's see if I've got this right," I said before he could

speak. "The grim reaper comes to collect someone but gets the name and the age back to front."

"Spot on," sighed Death.

"And you even got the town wrong."

"Right again."

"You should have got yourself a sat nav," I said, hoping he would understand the up-to-date references.

"Yeah, you're right. We used to have them but budget cuts have put a stop to that."

"Budget cuts?"

"Yes, they're downsizing all the time. I used to cover just the south east of England. Now it's the whole of England and Wales. I'm not that familiar with the north."

"What do you mean by downsizing?"

Death's shoulders slumped.

"There's not the demand for this anymore. So we have had to cut back over the past fifty years or so."

"That's bonkers," I said. "People die every day."

"Not like they used to," said Death sadly. "Back in the days you had plague, famine, disease, pestilence, and I was rushed off my feet. Then you had your wars, illnesses, disasters, both man-made and natural. It was all go, I can tell you. But now you've got better lifestyles, lots of good food and the medical advancement means you're all living too long."

"I'm not," I snapped. "If it wasn't for you I'd be at a

party chasing after a gorgeous girl. Not stuck here with some third-rate grim reaper. Dim reaper, more like.

"Okay, okay. Drop the sarcasm," said Death. "It's not as if this happens all the time. No one likes making mistakes."

I wasn't going to let him off the hook.

"Most people would forgive a mistake but not one that ends in their premature death," I said. "Meanwhile, some other bloke is pottering away enjoying life, enjoying years that are mine by rights. What's going to happen to me and what's going to happen to him?"

"Who?"

"Arthur Barrington. The bloke you should be talking to."

"Well, he's still alive, obviously. But it'll have to be a rush job to fit him in. It looks like it's going to be a late one tonight."

"Is that supposed to make me feel better?"

Death held up his bony hand.

"I'm sorry, Barry – can I call you Barry?"

I nodded.

"I was just trying to cheer you up," said Death. "I might look terrifying and spend my time snuffing out people's lives but it doesn't mean I don't have a sense of humour. Sometimes we have a bit of a laugh when I take them to the other side."

"Really?"

"Well, not all of them. Most of them are screaming and begging forgiveness, or in a catatonic silence."

"I'm not surprised."

"But I've got some good news for you, Barry. Head Office said I'll be able to put you back. It won't be at the exact time you died but it's the best I can do."

"That suits me," I said. "Bring it on."

"Before you go, mate, I'd just like to apologise for the mistake and the poor service you've had today. It's not the way we like to treat our clients. We pride ourselves on doing a good, professional job. Also, I want to thank you for your patience and understanding. And one day we'll make this journey together properly. I'll look forward to it."

"I won't. No offence."

"None taken. I promise I'll get it right next time. All the best. Bye."

It went black again. But not for long.

When I came to I was in bed, wrapped in the arms of a dark-haired girl. She kissed me gently on the nose and looked at me in a way that no other woman had done before. I had never seen such love and adoration in anyone's eyes.

And I felt the same way. My heart swelled with love for this woman. I was overwhelmed. I was about to let her know how I felt, to pour everything out, to tell her that no one else had ever made me feel this way.

But a nurse pushed her face right into mine.

"Oh, what a lovely little boy," she cooed. "Have you got a name for him yet?"

The dark-haired woman never took her eyes from mine.

"I'm thinking of calling him Barry," she said.

Marilyn's Letters
By Ann Taylor

To the Editor, *the Horton Advertiser*

Dear Sir,

I thought I would write and alert the readers of this newspaper to the fact that Mason Road will be closed due to water mains work. This is an abomination of poor planning on behalf of the Highways Department as Mason Road was only dug up and closed last September for new fibre optic cables.

It now means I will have a long walk through East Street with its rain-filled potholes and litter-strewn grass. What a miserable prospect!

Marilyn W.

Dear Sir,

With ongoing repairs in Mason Road, I am forced to walk to Horton's one remaining supermarket via East Street where I notice the pub sign for the not-so-new New Inn is swinging precariously in the wind on one bracket. I have written to the owners as I am concerned that it may fall on the drunks and yobs, some of whom are young women, who fall out of there as early as 10 o'clock in the morning!

Doesn't anyone have anything to do nowadays?

Marilyn W.

Dear Sir,

Perhaps your correspondent, Marilyn W, would care to know that the reeling drunks who fall out of the New Inn at 10am are in fact attending a breakfast club for Horton Volunteers. The young women are mothers who meet for coffee and a chat, and organise quiz nights at the pub to raise money for St Peter's Primary. Perhaps she would care to join us at one of our events?

John S.

Dear Sir,

I notice that the deadline for finishing Mason Road has come and gone. Do contractors ever meet their deadlines? I have written to the council to express my disgust.

On a further note your correspondent John S mentioned St. Peter's Primary School. Has anyone else been bowled off their feet by the 4 x 4s belching their fumes as they tear down the diverted route of East Street to deliver their children to school?

In these days of childhood obesity and pollution wouldn't it benefit the children and the environment if more people walked? I have written to the Headmistress of St Peter's to suggest this.

Marilyn W.

Dear Sir,

Marilyn W (last week's letters page) is quite right to point out the pleasures of walking. A lovely route for the children to walk to St Peter's would be through Gledhow Vale. The primroses are delightful at this time of year.

John S.

Dear Sir,

Acting upon your correspondent John S's suggestion I took a walk along Gledhow Vale the other day as the weather seems to have abated at long last. My amble through the dell was spoilt by the eyesore of dog-poo bags hanging from the branches of the trees as if some thoughtless people imagined they were baubles to festoon a Christmas tree! Old cigarette packets were tossed among last autumn's leaves and there were two drinks cans floating in the stream by the bridge. I have written to the council. However, the primroses were wonderful and the bluebells under the beech trees should be out soon.

Marilyn W.

Dear Sir,

Your correspondent Marilyn W is quite right to point out that Gledhow Vale could do with a bit of a tidy up. It does seem to have got rather neglected over the winter months. However, she seems to have failed to see that the undergrowth which was cleared last year is now teeming with forget-me-nots.

Perhaps Marilyn W would care to meet me at 4pm this Friday on the bridge. I could show her the wild orchid meadow. I will be wearing a red baseball cap and perhaps she could also wear something red so that we can identify each other.

John S.

Dear Sir,

Mr John S (last week's letters) seems to think that I have nothing better to do with my time but meet strange men with baseball caps in the middle of the Vale! But since I would be walking on Friday anyhow, I thought I would venture that way around 4pm. I hate the colour red almost as much as I hate baseball caps but I managed to find an old maroon scarf which belonged to my late husband.

As I made my way past Mason Road, I was pleased to see that the workmen were at last removing the diversion signs. It has only taken five whole weeks of inconvenience!

On East Street there was a man on a ladder fixing the sign at the New Inn and another one giving the windows a much-needed coat of paint.

As I entered Gledhow Vale I noticed that a bin had been installed for dog owners' deposits. I intend to write to the council to point out that it is now overflowing with dog-poo bags and needs emptying more frequently.

However, my walk towards the bridge was litter-free and pleasant. Imagine my consternation then when this peace was disturbed by a bubble of voices coming from the bridge. Children were laughing and parents were calling them to order. Even greater was my amazement when I rounded the bend to see a whole horde of folk standing by the bridge. There they were – mothers idling under the azaleas with their pushchairs, men leaning over the bridge, chatting and children playing roly-poly on the grass banks. I counted at least ten people wearing baseball caps, some using litter pickers to fish cans from the stream Another contingent of red caps was mounting an assault on a mound of butt ends.

The row was enough to scare the birds away and I hope the wild orchids were not trampled to smithereens. I had never had so many people talking to me at once. I was quite exhausted.

Marilyn W.

Dear Sir,

I have been too busy to write to this Letters Page recently but feel I must make an urgent suggestion to your readers about the necessity of volunteering in the local community. I have only recently discovered this pleasure myself. On Tuesdays I attend St Peter's Primary School where I listen to the children read. I have also become the Secretary of the excellent Horton Volunteer Club which has done superb work in clearing Gledhow Vale. They are identified by their red baseball caps which I also deign to wear on occasions. They meet on Thursdays at 10am at the well-run New Inn pub on East Street. I hope to meet new recruits there soon.

Marilyn W.

The Fancy Dress Party
By Maisie Dance

Jane slammed the car bonnet down with an oath. Why on earth had she agreed to Richard's crazy idea for new year's eve. A Georgian fancy dress party at a country inn. And now this! Hitching up the long skirt she trudged down the snowy lane.

She had walked round two bends before she saw the pinprick of light through the now swirling snow. Breathing a sigh of relief as she turned into the driveway, Jane saw the old house had a flickering lamp in the porchway and on the oak door was a huge iron knocker.

She knocked and after a short while the door was opened by a tall, good-looking man also dressed in Georgian costume. He bowed.

"Ah, you must be one of my sister's intimates. Do come in." Jane saw he had brilliant blue eyes and a mocking smile.

"I must say I have always found Cissy's companions rather plain and strait-laced. Whereas you. . . forgive my manners. You are wet through and shivering. Did your carriage break down?"

Jane laughed. "You could say that!" She followed him into a room where a log fire glowed and candles in tall candlesticks gave a warm mellow light.

Deftly the man removed her sodden boots and cloak, rubbing her feet with his long slender hands. Jane felt her eyes close with the heat of the fire. This is much nicer than a boring fancy dress party. Her eyes snapped open. Richard! He would be waiting for her. And who on earth is Cissy?

"Can I use your phone?" she enquired, cursing the person who had snatched her mobile only the day before. The blank look answered her question. Evidently they were still living in the dark ages. "Only Richard, my friend. . ."

"The story of my life. A beautiful stranger comes to my door, the angel I have been looking for, and now I find she is betrothed to another." Jane felt herself blushing, something she hadn't done since her teens.

"You are going to the same party aren't you?" she asked. "Only, he will be getting worried."

Just then the door opened and a young girl

entered, also dressed in costume. "Who is this you're entertaining, Phillip? I didn't know we were expecting. . ."

The dark eyebrows shot up. "You mean this delectable lady is not one of your companions? Well I did say I had never met any who weren't plain and prudish. . ."

"Phillip! I am sorry my brother is forgetful of his manners. Please introduce us."

"Ah. I'm afraid I have been lax. I only know she is sadly betrothed to Richard. . ."

"Richard! Well that explains it. He said he was bringing his intended. Now, he will be waiting impatiently. Are you ready to go, Miss. . ."

"Jane Tilbright, and yes I am quite ready if you have room for me."

"Of course. The carriage is waiting."

Jane was astonished to find a carriage with horses and a coachman waiting at the gate. Wasn't this taking fancy dress too far? She found herself tucked in a rug with Phillip beside her. Cissy chatted away from her seat opposite them as they bowled along through the snowy night, the lamps lighting up trees and an occasional cottage along the way. Jane tensed as she found Phillip's hand holding hers under the rug, and then relaxed and let it stay.

At last brilliant lights appeared ahead as other carriages jostled for position by the large front door. Jane was helped down from the carriage and escorted into a huge room lit by candelabras. Everyone she saw was in Georgian costume. And she recognised no one. Phillip touched her arm.

"Ah, here is Richard come to claim you." He pointed to a fair-haired man approaching them. "Richard, I really think you should take more care of your intended!"

A woman swept up to him and laid a possessive hand on his arm. "His intended? What is this, Richard?"

He looked quizzically down on Jane, then turning to Phillip he said, "This is my intended, Phillip. This is my beloved Bella, and although I can see your companion is very beautiful, my heart is already taken." Bowing, he strolled off.

"I think," Jane said faintly, "this is the wrong party."

Phillip smiled down at her. "I have never heard such good news. Come and dance, my darling."

The sky was turning pink with the coming dawn when Jane and Phillip left. He had manoeuvred her on to the terrace, where he had kissed her until she was reeling. Jane was floating on air.

Soon, they were back in the carriage, with a sleepy coachman at the front, trotting through the country lanes. Jane nestled her head against Phillip's shoulder.

"When does the carriage turn into a pumpkin, Phillip?" He kissed her forehead then murmured, "Shall

I let you go, dear Jane, or would you be willing to spend your life with me, forsaking all others?"

Jane looked up into his intense eyes and breathed, "Oh yes, Phillip. Although we've only just met, I never dreamed I could feel like this."

The carriage stopped at the gate of the old house and Phillip lifted her down, pulling her into his arms and kissing her again and again. At first the kiss was as before, burning with passion, but all at once Jane felt her lips burning not with heat but with intense cold. She gasped, pushing feebly against his chest, but Phillip continued to kiss her until her lips turned blue.

Gently he laid her on the path.

· · ·

They found her on new year's day, outside the derelict Georgian house.

"Poor young woman, she must have frozen to death last night. Look, there's still icicles on her lips."

"Aye well, I'm not staying here. They say that old house is haunted on new year's eve."

Kiteflying on Aranmore
By Tina Enlander

A whim brings us to Aranmore. "You've talked about it long enough," says Joe. So we go, late in August when summer was still holding on by its fingertips.

"Dry but breezy," promised the weather lady. I cling to an image of a perfect day, a Greek idyll of forty, yes it was forty, years ago.

Last-minute packing, nothing planned, piles thrown on the back seat. It's just us, no clamorous offspring spread about. Still it all mounts, clothes for all weathers, food and drink, the dog biscuits and bowl in a plastic bag. Don't forget to put the dog in the boot. Collie dog to Collie Island as it turns out.

From east coast to west, it's not too far but far enough for change. Leaving things behind, the trappings. Vodafone texts 'You are roaming' like vagabonds loose on the road.

Crossing the border, invisible line but so portent. We shrug off our 'cares and woes' singing out tunelessly.

"When will you get the radio fixed?"

"No time," he replies.

I wheeze against the sore throat and sinus that has attacked my ears. Sick on holiday, it's become a trend, my body playing tricks. Age!

Miles are eaten up as we crest the hills above Dunloe. Atlantic view, grey, clouds skimming the sky. Dry and breezy.

The ferry runs in most weathers, the guide book states. It's because of the sheltered bay and all those islets. "Where did they come from?" I ask aloud. "They weren't there forty years ago."

Joe glances quizzically and shakes his head.

I don't recall the road to Burtonport hitchhiked all in a group. We were 17, nice girls, sensible. Virgins without fear.

Burtonport is closed, shored up, broken down. No tea room, craft shop or maritime museum. The road's end, a steep concrete slipway. Cars wait, wipers on and off in the drizzle. The boatman choreographs us as we each perform an arc and reverse slowly on to the deck. Mirrors folded back like clipped wings, three rows, tucked in, stowed and ship-shaped following the contours of the red Aranmore ferry.

Twenty minutes from Burtonport to the island. No distance but time collapses like a telescope. Forty years! I don't recall the crossing then, us girls standing on the upper deck in the gold sunlight. I was blonder, hair lifting in the breeze, facing forward, a figure on the prow. That was how it must have been, then.

Now I stand in the well of the boat, Collie dog straining to peer through a porthole, looking back to Donegal, the islets slipping by. I still don't remember them. A blue ferry meets us, passes, a single car on board. No waving but a nod, a raised finger, the Donegal way.

"Are you going for the country music festival?" Daniel O' Daniel look-a-likes, matrons in cardigans, freshly primped and preened steal into view.

"No, we are not." Too late to turn back, we are committed.

Not so dry now but the wind has dropped. Bunting hangs slack and brazen. Welcome back, it signals secretly.

There it is! The hostel, no longer An Oige, now a backpackers' rest, desirable residence. Still the fabric is there in square, blunt mortar. Now dull with rain. Then summer lit, our hopeful eyes brighter, keen.

The curved pale shore is bare of footprints but ghosts hover dimly where the marron grass banks. A green mound where we sat, chords plucked by air so long ago. Thin laughter recedes like the waves. I shrug off this nostalgia returning to the us who are now.

Follow the chart, turn left then right up the hill. The holiday village, rural suburbia – no parties, no Hen or Stag groups, no need for a deposit. We look like we can be trusted. Models of middle age.

"So you are here for the country music then?"

"No," we retort in unison, a need to assert ourselves, not to be judged by our cover. We are capable of mischief!

Were we so wild then or did we just seem the part? Lovely lasses seeking romance, fond looks, a caress? Nothing unvirginal, we were good convent girls.

Nothing nun-like now, this body, maternal monument. Babies conceived, carried, born.

"Will we go for a walk?" He hovers into view. This man, Joe, father to our children, not known forty years ago. His feet are new to this place while mine remember.

The lane dips gently to the sea. Collie dog wags enthusiastically, meandering down, silvered muzzle, amber eyes. That's her name, Amber, eyes once shining now matted to a rich sheen.

These are new scents, intriguing smells. As we round the shoreline, four black and white dogs greet us, stick ready for throwing. Four Collie dogs on an adventure. Our dog slopes into the pack, now there are five. Five Collie dogs on Aranmore!

Island time lingers as the light fades. Nine o'clock,

mark of autumn. It is nearly dark.

"What will we do tomorrow?" he asks.

Let's see what the weather is up to.

"Intermittent showers but warm, no noticeable breeze." We'll go to the lighthouse on the other side. It's good to have a plan.

I dream of Collie dogs on the shore. I throw the stick over and over again. In and out of the water, ecstatic, alert. Free doggy spirits. Were we like that, the giddy girls, water sprites, sirens of the sea quenching our thirst for life? Carpe diem, each and every day seized and squeezed of all it could give?

I wake to silence and mist. "There's a Snowy Owl in the hills. We'll look for it on our way." This is new territory, a place neither of us own, new memories to share when we talk of the island. Ours not mine.

The Snowy Owl glows white against the turf cutting, iridescent, its beak a lethal razor, its feathers an ermine cloak. It is alone, alien, both sad and magnificent. Why is it here? Is it lost? Can it survive? "It's from Iceland," Joe informs me. Young single male spreading its wings before mating. I think of Norse sagas, tales of exploration, the search for self. Islands seem the place to be when you are young and free.

The owl turns its head in an almost complete circle and looks straight at us. Arrogant youth!

The trail is boulder-strewn and pitted with holes. Driving is slowed as we inch to a point on the map; here is a lake, bent trees, a moor. The lighthouse squats inelegantly, a walled enclosure setting it apart. Sheep crop the meadow-topped cliffs. Atlantic rollers uncurl against the basalt below, sky is blue and peerless above. A lark sings.

"What's this?" Joe asks, lifting a polythene pouch from the car. "A kite," I reply. "I'm going to fly it." Kiteflying on Aranmore.

I see the kite, neon colours rising, soaring as it fills with air, splendid beacon. In my imagination I see it.

"It won't fly, there's not enough wind!" We stand facing each other, the length of the kite string separating us. Joe lifts the lifeless fabric above his head. We wait, I with the two lines in my hands.

This is an island, a headland, the edge. It is wind-parched!

"Leave it," Joe says as he walks off. The dog is bemused. Stay or follow, mistress or master?

I lay out the kite, its shrouds neatly spread, backing away almost reverentially. I am poised to catch a breath, even a murmur of air.

Sheep congregate, curiosity a brief interlude to grazing. The dog shifts, nosing the unfamiliar peat. Another skylark. There is no wind, there will be no kite flying today.

"We can try again," Joe says when I catch up with him. Perhaps another time.

We say goodbye to Aranmore, easing the car into the hold. Goodbye harbour, the Ferry cafe, the little shop beside the pub. I forget to look for the hostel.

Four Collie dogs run along the beach chasing a colourful piece of cloth. It flutters, balloons like a spinnaker and is gone, rainbow fading like a chord.

The Date
By Sandy Vaughan

As soon as she walked into the pub she spotted him. He was sitting at a table in the bay window, watching the door. He stood as she approached.

"Alex," she said. It was a statement rather than a question.

"Karen," he replied in a gentle voice, and with a wave indicated a seat.

She had studied his photo, read his history carefully, and folded in her bag was the printout from the internet dating site. But nothing had prepared her for his gut-wrenching gorgeousness. He was, quite simply, beautiful and totally desirable.

For a few long, disbelieving moments, she simply stared. A cloud of bright butterflies flitted through her stomach. Everything about him was stunning and unsettling. Could this really be him, the man she'd been looking for, for so long?

"Drink?" he asked, breaking her reverie.

"Oh yes, I'll just have a shandy, I'm driving.'"

When he went to the bar she allowed herself to breathe again. His instant and overwhelming sexual attraction had unnerved her. Karen imagined herself as one of those cartoon characters with a little demon on one shoulder whispering love at first sight, and a little angel on the opposite shoulder shouting stop it, stop it, stop it.

Over their drinks they compared notes on their respective divorces. They gently boasted of their children's achievements and of their endearing or frustrating habits.

When her phone jingled, her response was brusque. "Yes. Yes of course. I'll leave here at 10.30," and she hit End Call. He raised a questioning eyebrow.

"My daughter, checking when I'll be back tonight." The lie didn't sit easily with her and colour rose to her cheeks.

She didn't hear much of his conversation, aware only of the firestorm of conflicting desire and repulsion raging through her. Her heart raced as she fantasised about him running his fingers through her hair and caressing her neck. Those imaginings were immediately chased away by dark fears and disbelief that she could possibly be sitting here and wanting him.

"I don't want to be on my own any more," she heard

him say, "I get lonely. But all the women I've met recently didn't want to stay, and I tried very hard to keep them."

She checked her watch, 10 o'clock. It wasn't yet too late. She could suggest they drive to a wine bar somewhere, and perhaps afterwards on to – where?

He continued to talk, she continued not to listen, deafened by the roar of adrenaline-powered blood pumping through her veins.

It was 10.30. A lump rose in her chest.

"Will you walk me to my car?" she asked, reaching out and closing her fingers over his. He raised her hand to his lips and murmured her name. Never breaking eye contact, together they rose from the table.

As they stepped through the door she briefly shut her eyes, then slipped her fingers out of his.

Out of the darkness an arm reached around her and she was pulled aside.

A fast-moving shape rammed Alex into the wall. Another forced his arms behind his back.

As the handcuffs were locked around his wrists she heard the first words of the recited caution, "Alex Griffiths, I am arresting you on suspicion of the abduction and rape of Eliza Matthews, the abduction and rape of Sarah Hurst. . ."

Karen turned away in silence and walked towards her unmarked car.

Matthew on Thursdays
By Rita Houghton

The secret of making a good cup of tea was to have absolutely boiling water, a warm teapot and proper tea, not tea bags. This was the procedure my mother had passed on to me and she should know.

I sighed. Now there was only myself to make tea for since Graham had passed on. I felt the familiar signs of despondency creeping over me at the thought of the lonely days and nights ahead. *Stop being so self-pitying*, I told myself. *It's Matthew on Thursday.* The thought made me feel a lot better.

Matthew had been sent by some body called The Association For Ex-Prisoners Re-entry Into Society. An earnest young man called Mr Partridge came to see me. "You see Mrs Dodds our people [he meant the ex-prisoners] need an opportunity to prove they're ready to return to society. Perhaps a little gardening?" he said.

The church I attend had some liaison with the association so I'd felt obliged to comply, although my garden is miniscule and I can easily manage it myself.

"I'd like to help but would it be safe?" I asked doubtfully. I had visions of shaved heads and uniforms with arrows like Magwitch in *Great Expectations*.

"Perfectly safe. Matthew has served his time and I'm sure you'll find him a very likeable young chap."

"Can you tell me what Matthew was, er, in for?" I couldn't think of any other way to put it.

Mr Partridge made a prim mouth. "We have found, in all fairness, that it's best if past misdemeanours aren't initially revealed. That way there are no pre-conceptions. Rest assured Mrs Dodds, you'll be quite safe with Matthew."

It was arranged that Matthew would begin on the following Thursday for two hours. On no account was I to offer him monetary reward.

"Splendid then." Mr Partridge's folder was slapped shut.

By Wednesday I had all but made up my mind to cancel the arrangements but in the end I lost courage.

Matthew didn't look at all like Magwitch. His hair was fair and floppy, framing a thin pale face. He wore blue jeans and an imitation leather bomber jacket with not an arrow in sight. After Mr Partridge left,

I awkwardly offered Matthew a cup of tea, my panacea for everything.

"After you've had your tea, I'll show you where I keep the tools, maybe you can start by sweeping up the leaves and making a bonfire." I hoped he hadn't been in jail for arson.

After that Matthew came every Thursday and the first thing I did was to make us a cup of tea.

"Tea for two and two for tea," he'd warble and always make me laugh about something or other. Sometimes he'd impersonate Mick Jagger or another pop star and we'd both fall apart laughing.

In the beginning, I'd locked away everything of any value but quickly gave that up. One Thursday before the end of his term with me, I asked him why he'd been sent to prison.

"Armed robbery except it wasn't," he hastened as my eyes widened in alarm. "I was desperate for money. Couldn't get a job and no prospects so I held up this garage. I had my hands in my pockets, like this." He thrust them into his pockets to demonstrate. "The garage attendant must have thought I had a gun and pressed the alarm. Before I knew it the police were all over the place and bang, into jail I went. First offence though so they went easy on me."

"Aren't there people who can help if you're desperate?"

My idea of desperation was hazy.

"Hundreds of unemployed out there Mrs D. It worked out okay though. I'm going to the training centre to learn to be a plumber. In demand plumbers are."

"That's good then." I sat back and inspected him from behind my tea cup. "Maybe it's not my place to say but I couldn't help noticing the watch you wear. I mean it's not really in keeping with your circumstances." I'd spotted the fine gold watch the very first day.

"This?" He held his wrist up. "I didn't steal it if that's what you're thinking. It was my Dad's. The only real thing of value he had. He never had any money, only had this and he gave it to me before he died. Many's the time I thought of selling or pawning it but I never did. Glad I didn't now."

The last Thursday of the month arrived and with it the last time Matthew would be coming to me.

"I'll miss you," I said, giving the tea an extra stir.

"You've been good to me Mrs D. Always trusted me even after what I told you."

"Well you served your time and learnt your lesson I'm sure."

Just before four o'clock he came into the kitchen, a worried frown creasing his face.

"I can't find my watch anywhere. I took it off to wash at the tap and can't remember seeing it again."

"Are you sure?" I asked urgently.

"I've looked all over the flower beds, even the gravel drive."

"The compost heap?" I asked hopefully.

He shook his head. "There too. I can't believe I've lost it."

We both went into the garden to search but it proved fruitless; the watch had indeed disappeared.

"I promise, I'll look every day," I said and put my arms around his slim frame to give him a tentative hug.

With his head down Matthew walked off down the street a picture of hopeless dejection, leaving me at the gate waving until he was out of sight.

A cup of tea was called for. As I waited for the kettle to boil I pattered upstairs to my bedroom and unlocked the drawer of my dressing table. It was a lovely Swiss watch, I thought.

My fingers wandered over a brooch in the shape of an owl with two glittering amber eyes. That had belonged to dear Muriel Devereux from the WI. A lace handkerchief and hand printed silk scarf had been from the vicar's wife, a lovely lady.

Graham had made me go to see someone about my acquisitive habit and they had come up with some mad-sounding name which meant I couldn't resist helping myself to other people's things.

Graham had lectured me and told me stealing was very wrong and had to stop. "It isn't stealing," I told him. Imagine calling me a thief. Why, that would put me in the same category as Mr Partridge's people. "It's just I like to have little keepsakes of people I'm fond of."

Sighing I lay the watch with my other memories. It is sad how people come and go out of your life. I will really miss Matthew on Thursdays.

Perhaps I should ring Mr Partridge on Monday and ask for another helper; after all it is in a good cause.

I make my way downstairs to enjoy my cup of tea and perhaps a biscuit too.

Flames
By Lindsey Malin

It was chilly in the sitting room. Draughts were coming under the closed doors and from the windows. Sometimes when it was very cold outside, the condensation made frost patterns on the inside of the window panes – flowers, ferns and leaves in sparkling white. But there was no warmth in the room now and the grate in the centre of the long wall was empty and bare.

She made some spills the way her grandmother had taught her, moistening the corner of a double page of newspaper with spittle, rolling it up tightly and bending it into a sculptural knot which was as effective as a piece of kindling. A number of these were laid on top of the bunched up newssheet in the grate. On them she carefully placed a few pieces of chopped wood, chunky and rough, and finally some lumps of coal, making sure they didn't fall.

Now the edifice was ready and she dusted off her hands. Taking a match she struck it, held it against the newspaper at the bottom of the pile and watched as the flames crept round and inwards. There was a faint crackling noise. The sudden life mesmerised her. Fire flared up against the loosely packed paper and started to char the spills. It was a creation.

The flames made patterns and unexpected movements against the background of the grate. The room appeared a little more welcoming now. There was enough paper at the bottom of the pile for the fire to keep going until the spills had caught alight. With a slight feeling of trepidation she reached for a large double sheet of newspaper and carefully placed it over the chimney opening with a few inches overlap at the sides and top holding it in place to keep the air out. The grill below the grate was open and uncovered, and almost at once the air came surging through to feed the fire with oxygen.

She had to hang on tightly to the paper as the vacuum sucked it inwards. This sudden rush of air encouraged the spills to smoulder strongly and the pieces of wood began to catch alight reluctantly at first then with more energy. At the same time a roaring started and an orange glow appeared behind the newssheet. The fire was spreading, but taking the paper away too soon would cause it to die back, and the entire procedure would have to be done again. However if it became too strong the paper could easily catch alight. The roar became louder and she could make out the shape of the flames flickering behind the newspaper, the inner light growing brighter and more persistent. A sense of danger made her whisk away the paper now, deftly, so it didn't touch the fire which was now burning healthily without any help. The wood had caught and was playing around the coal which had begun to smoulder. A few more lumps would help draw the flames.

A small cloud of smoke had escaped when she had removed the paper and the smell of the burning wood and coal lingered in the room. The flames purred and danced, burning merrily now, and threw up restless patterns in the grate. The tinge of blue playing round the coal flowered into orange shapes constantly changing and moving. The warmth began to permeate the room.

Each Day as it Comes
By Gwenda Major

As Frances peeled the delicate pink strips from the stick of rhubarb her attention drifted outside where the sight of the empty window boxes reproached her. By now, she thought, Tom would have had the boxes planted up with bold red geraniums. He always used red flowers at this time of year, loved the contrast they made with the grey limestone of the house. A reassuring annual display that heralded the arrival of summer and long days in the garden. But not this year.

It was nearly a year already since Tom's death, a year since she had said goodbye to him in the hospice, holding his hand until his rasping breathing stopped and peace had settled on the light-filled room. It had almost been a relief in the end, the death Frances had dreaded for so long; all those interminable months of watching him fade, fail to recognise her, become helpless.

"At least it wasn't a shock," well-meaning people would say in the weeks after he died as if that made it all right, acceptable. "Take each day as it comes," others said. Or, "you've still got your memories," and Frances would smile and thank them, trying to remind herself they meant well.

As friends had predicted, the numbness of the first few days had seen her through the arrangements and the funeral allowed her to greet people, read the cards that came with every post and reassure the children she was fine. It was only weeks later that Frances began to see Tom. He sat next to her in the car as she went shopping, stood at her shoulder as she loaded the dishwasher, lay beside her in bed at night. She spoke to him aloud, berating him for leaving her, accusing him of selfishness and neglect. She almost expected him to answer her.

But the worst time came later, a couple of months after Tom died, as summer faded. Frances had gone back to work by then and colleagues had mostly stopped mentioning Tom, hinting that she must want to "get back to normal". A pall of quiet sadness had settled over her and she went through the motions of daily life passively, sitting silently in meetings, staring mindlessly at the computer screen, dully listening to clients' problems. In the evenings she dug out old photo albums and turned pages back to a time when Tom was fit and well, riding a bike and waving at the camera, lifting one of the children up in his arms to watch a firework display, paddling a canoe on a French camping trip.

She almost began to look forward to the tears as they fell each night, the sharp pain as she looked at Tom's smiling face.

Cassie arrived one evening to find her mother surrounded by photo albums, weeping helplessly. "Mum, this is no good. You're depressed. You've got to put all these photos away. You're just making it worse dwelling on the past like this."

Brisk no-nonsense Cassie tidied her up as she tidied her patients on the ward and made her promise to leave the albums in the cupboard and "get out more". Dutifully Frances tried, accepted a couple of invitations – to a meal out, a theatre trip, but her heart was not in it. She wanted to be back at home with Tom, sifting her memories, letting the hours spool in yearning and regret.

She tried to be clear and truthful in her remembering, looking at the bad times as well as the good. The time she was convinced Tom was having an affair but had never confronted him. Was he? She had never known for sure and now never would. The time Charlie had dropped out of university and she and Tom had argued helplessly about why he had done it and what they should do, blaming each other bitterly. In the end Charlie had sorted himself out, seemed successful and happy now. Frances re-played their marital sulks and silences as well as their joys and shared pleasures as if she felt she needed to memorise their life together before she could let it go.

Down at the bottom of the steep garden was a dense, high leylandii hedge, and beyond that a public footpath that led to the next village. One day in May Frances went down the garden to do some digging and stopped after half an hour to rest on the bench Tom had bought her for their thirtieth anniversary. Through the hedge she heard the rhythmic panting of a dog, then a little while later the soft whirring of bike wheels and then the plaintive hiccupping of a distressed child. The sounds moved along the hedge and faded. *Life is passing me by*, Frances thought. *I am here but not part of it all. I should be moving on, getting involved but I don't know how.* She stared helplessly at the pile of weeds she had pulled up as if they might provide the answer.

The next morning the dawn chorus woke Frances and she lay at peace listening to the delicate tracery of sound. Her limbs felt heavy, comfortably surrendered to the bed. Then she remembered it was Saturday and Cassie and Ed were coming round for an evening meal so she forced herself to get up and dressed to go out.

In town she saw a poster for a lunchtime organ recital in the parish church. Frances decided to go. She had only been inside the church a few times but remembered the wide generous nave and the vibrant stained glass. Less than twenty people were seated inside and Frances slipped quietly into a pew towards the back and waited, her thoughts still and peaceful.

Suddenly the organ burst out with the beginning of Bach's Toccata and Fugue in D Minor. Ladders of bright sound rose to the roof of the church. Frances held her breath. She looked up and saw how the improbable carved angels on the roof beams seemed to have paused in flight to listen. She smiled as the music swelled and shook the old building. She had forgotten the wonder of music, the power of rhythms and patterns of sounds. She felt suddenly full of life and energy.

At home she unloaded the groceries then opened up the shed. First she scooped handfuls of potting compost into the big round stone pot on the garden wall and packed it with the bright yellow pansies she had bought. Finally, smiling to herself, Frances rotated the bowl so that the pansies already seemed to have turned their faces to the soft summer sun.

Stella's a Star
By Jean Duggleby

I've had a visitor today, in fact two visitors, Mike and Stella. And they might be the answer to my problems.

Mike is the usual besuited businessman but he explained it very clearly and left me with the paperwork to look at.

Stella is a tall blond with lovely long legs wearing the shortest of miniskirts. She's for the sex trade which I don't think I want, but I can use the model of my choice. I'm going for middle-aged, motherly with kind eyes and a ready smile – a bit like my daughter who lives in New Zealand.

It's expensive and you can't get it on the NHS. But I've been careful with money all my life and at the age of 93 I have quite a lot of savings.

There's nothing wrong with my mind. But my body's falling to bits. I sometimes can't get to the loo in time and that's very embarrassing. I can't reach high shelves or pick up my heavier saucepans. I haven't been able to get the lids off jars or open tins for years.

You hear stories of helpers conning old people into giving their life savings. I know an old man who had his car stolen by his carers. You even hear of old people getting bashed up. It's all so scary.

Stella doesn't need a bedroom, just a cupboard where she can be plugged in for recharging. I'll get her for a trial run next week.

. . .

Well, it's been wonderful. She's so patient and doesn't even get cross when I wet the bed. She's a great cook and helps me with my flower arranging. Stella means 'star' and she is certainly that.

She can drive apparently but we use Dial-a-Ride and now I can get out and about.

I even get some human visitors these days and I think it's because I'm better company. I don't moan all the time.

I'm definitely going to keep her.

. . .

One day, a few months after Stella moved in, a young man came to the door saying he wanted to read the electricity meter. He had the uniform, the badge and all. Once he was in he let two other men in and they herded the two of us into the kitchen. They all had knives. They demanded money, my jewellery and antiques, Stella's mobile phone and our card details.

When we refused, one made a lunge at me with his knife. Stella with one beautiful move kicked the knife out of his hand and kneed him in the groin leaving him groaning on the floor.

Another one plunged his knife into where Stella's heart would have been if she'd had one. She pulled the knife out herself and slit his throat with it. The third one started to do a runner but she grabbed his legs and he fell over hitting his head on a cupboard.

She quickly told me to find the kitchen string. I haven't moved so fast in years. Within minutes she had them all tied up. I even helped by putting my finger on the knots. It was so exciting.

They all survived, even the one with the slit throat. It took a while to sort it out with all the police reports and going to court but it's finished now. They're banged up in prison.

Thank goodness I chose the self-defence model.

A Winter's Tale
By Peter Lewis

The snow came at dusk, heavy and silent. A man, stumbling into the clearing of a dense forest, saw a weak light emanating from a hovel. Frozen, he knocked at the door and a feeble voice cried, "Who's there?"

"A soldier of the King's army, madam. Jack Randall by name. Please let me shelter awhile. I'm close to dying of cold and exhaustion."

The bolt was slowly dragged across and the door creaked half open. The old woman looked closely for a few moments at the man, who was indeed a soldier and a wounded one at that, and then said, "Enter if you mean me no harm."

"Thank ye kindly, ma'am. I mean you no harm at all. Bless ye for giving me shelter this wicked night. My blood is near freezing."

"You're wounded bad. What happened to you?"

"Oh, 'tis naught. A scrape. After the battle two days ago I was separated from my troop and attacked by cut-throats. I stuck my knife into one and did for him but the other came at me from behind thinking to finish me. He was no fighter and I left him for dead. Do you have a bite to eat, please you, ma'am?"

Jack sat and watched the bent old woman as she bustled about the room, stirring up the fire, putting more logs on and swinging a soot-encrusted cauldron over it. Soon there was a pungent but not unpleasant smell of broth.

She's a right old crone, thought Jack. *Ugly as the grave. Methinks I shan't be disturbing her this night. Not that I have the energy, though she's kind enough.*

"You're very gracious, ma'am, this is indeed tasty. What do they call you?"

"I have no use for names but you may call me Lady, for once I was one, though 'tis hard to believe now."

As Jack was finishing his soup and a hunk of stale black bread, he was falling asleep. The woman put down fresh straw with a threadbare rug on top in a corner of the hut, and gestured Jack to lie there. Just before she blew out her solitary candle he noticed she took a small leather pouch from under her voluminous skirts and swiftly hid it under her pillow. He watched her drop noisily into bed in the flickering firelight. Then he slept soundly for many hours until hunger gnawed him awake and he sat up wondering where he was. He thought he had dreamt last night's meeting but then he smelled the broth in the cauldron and remembered.

There was no sign of Lady. He presumed she was gathering firewood and, taking an ancient cracked bowl from a shelf, he helped himself to some of the broth. As he ate he mused that perhaps he might spend some time here if the old crone would let him. He was sure she could be persuaded to look after him. Then he thought, *Perhaps not. I'm too fond of a pretty skirt or two to stay in this godforsaken hole.*

Looking across at her unmade bed he remembered the pouch she had put under her pillow and wondered if it was still there. In one stride he was at the bed and had lifted the pillow. It was there and he swiftly opened it. What he saw made him whistle softly. "God's blood. This is a mighty fine piece of jewellery."

What he held in his hand was about the size of his thumbnail, shaped like a lozenge and deep blue in colour. Light as a raindrop, it gave off a lustrous pale sheen and Jack thought, *I'll have this. The old crone can't have any use for it. Mayhap I can give up soldiering when I sell this and live like the King I serve.* Peering out through the door and seeing the old crone's footsteps leading away to the left he made his escape. Slipping and sliding over the fresh snow, he failed to notice the old woman, crouching at the back of the hovel, cackling her satisfaction.

Six months went by and Jack had all but forgotten his night in the forest and the old crone, but as he stood at the altar looking at the beauty he had just married, with the jewel set in a silver clasp on her breast, he remembered and shivered as, momentarily, his bride's face became the crone's face. He blinked and all was as it should be again.

Jack hadn't needed to sell the jewel. He was treated as a hero by the King when he returned to duty, saying the men he had killed in the forest were spies intent on murdering him and his bodyguards, and he was showered with gifts. He was made a captain and wooed and won the heart of the daughter of a fellow officer, with the gift of a splendid house as her dowry, and was looking forward to making her truly his wife.

At last the wedding feast was over and he and his bride lay side by side in bed, whispering words of love. The jewel lay on her neck, seeming to pulse, exciting him greatly. He leant across her and, kissing her full on the lips, whispered, "Are ye ready for a night of passion?"

She murmured "Yes," but it wasn't her voice. Jack opened his eyes and saw to his horror that his beautiful bride was changed, was changing before his very eyes. As the jewel glistened on her neck her face was ageing, her long auburn tresses were now a listless pale straw, deep frown lines were at her eyes and mouth, and her teeth were blackening even as she reached up to kiss him. Before he was even half out of bed she was the old crone from the forest. As Jack bolted from the bedroom he heard a terrifying cackle. He stumbled at the top of the stairs, fell heavily to the bottom and lay very still.

The Girl by the Wall
By Jane Varley

The girl was there again. Sitting at the foot of the wall. Her pale, oval face expressionless. Still, composed. Begging silently, a small bowl placed on the paving stone by her feet. Virginia creeper hung over the old stones and climbed the blue and gold wrought-iron railings behind her. The girl did not look up.

Ruth walked briskly by on her way to the bank. She had an old shopping bag heavy with coins from the university library's vending machine. She had sorted the cash into 10s, 20s, 50s, £1s and then counted it into neat piles. She had checked and double-checked the total amounts – it could be as much as £100 if she left it over a week. Then she'd put each denomination into a marked plastic bag.

Her bag was always heavy. Carrying it along the street made her feel self-conscious; she was sure everyone she passed saw the mousey little secretary scuttling along the pavement with a bag full of money.

On her next mission to the bank Ruth hoped the girl wouldn't be there. But she was there. Ruth fixed her eyes firmly on the pavement and concentrated on not walking on the cracks between the paving slabs. She was safe if she kept within bounds.

As autumn approached, the leaves of the virginia creeper began to show crimson tips and the air had a sharper quality. It was term-time again at the university and Ruth had to empty the vending machine more frequently. She always counted the coins, arranging the piles in neat rows, and she mentally translated each pile into a bowl of hot soup, a fresh baguette, a roasted vegetable sandwich.

What would the girl by the wall do with a couple of stacks of 10p coins? Would she buy food? Or drugs, more likely? Ruth heard a voice in her head warning against the folly of giving to street beggars, *It supports their vices. Much better to give it to a homeless charity. They do excellent work.*

When Ruth got to the corner of the road where the girl usually sat she flicked a nervous glance ahead of her. The girl was there looking pinched and cold. Ruth fingered the few coins she had deep in her coat pocket. But if she gave the girl something, she might come to expect a donation every time Ruth passed. And it would be such a little donation – goodness knows – Ruth's salary only just covered her own outgoings. She briskly crossed over to the other side of the road – and hated herself.

When she came out of the bank she almost tripped over a row of outstretched legs in ragged jeans. A pallid face leered at her from under spiked, painted hair and ring-pierced eyebrows; a filthy hand shot towards her. "Spare some change?" a voice whined. She was glad the money was safely in the bank.

Ruth walked on purposefully, treading in the squares and avoiding other walkers. Voices clamoured in her head. *Beggars are an eyesore on the streets of our towns and cities. Anyone in our society who wants a job can find one. The government makes adequate provision for cases of genuine hardship. Begging is unnecessary.* But Ruth knew that an unemployed teenager with no fixed address would receive nothing. She knew how difficult it was to get a job if you didn't have an address. She knew the monthly cost of an address.

Back at work the image of the girl sitting motionless and expressionless stayed with Ruth for days. A silent anger possessed her. It was not the fault of all the street beggars that they lived and begged and died on the streets. The system was at fault. Society was at fault. The individual was at fault. Ruth was at fault.

Her conscience weighed as heavy on her as the burden of the coins in her bag. The money which she carried faithfully to the bank went into the account of a vast and thriving corporation whose boss received a huge salary, no doubt. The obscenity of vast, uncountable sums accruing to one man appalled Ruth.

She thought of the pale girl by the wall. What if she should give her the coins next time she passed?

Ruth felt a creeping excitement; her skin tingled and her pulse pounded deafeningly in her ears. She could and would do something to redress the imbalance. She would make a gesture and accept whatever consequences came from it. She would step out of bounds. She had thought about it for days.

She had decided. She became obsessed by the plan. She was mesmerised by the simplicity of it – the sheer compulsion of it.

Next emptying time Ruth tipped the coins onto her desk. With measured calm she counted them into piles, 10s, 20s, 50s, £1s. There were many piles. The piles went into the bags and the bags went into the shopper. Her hands were sweating and she smelt the acrid metal on her clammy palms.

She strode out of the library elated, absorbed by her mission. Her feet trod on the cracks and on the squares. She gripped the handle of her bag till her nails dug into her hand. A feeling of weightlessness floated her along, she felt herself invisible.

In fifty steps she would be at the corner. She would see the girl sitting by the wall in the weak autumn sunlight. She would look into the girl's clear, empty eyes. There would be no reaction. She would drop the shopper with the money, all of it, at the girl's feet. On behalf of those who had, she would give to those who had not.

Ruth rounded the corner and cast her eyes forward, through the throng of passers-by to the place at the foot of the wall where the girl always sat. The crimson leaves of the creeper had already begun to drop onto the paving stones. They littered the pavement and danced a little circular dance in a breath of passing wind.

Round and round the brilliant leaves twirled at the foot of the old wall. On the paving stones. On the vacant paving stone. . . there was no girl.

The leaves blew against the wall in a trembling heap, lifted and rose up and passed through the blue and gold railings into the park beyond.

Ruth stood, her feet rooted to the exact centre of a large grey paving stone. Her moment of resolve had been snatched from her. A feeling of great loss overwhelmed her.

Pedestrians were jostling her and she became aware of the weight of the bag in her hand. She turned and walked to the kerb, carefully avoiding the cracks in the paving slabs. Then looking first right, then left, then right again she crossed the road to the bank.

Going Somewhere
By Beth Wildberry

So cold and wet and dark.

The Red Cross lady flashed a torch over the shiny pavements. It was a long walk from the train.

Where were they going? "You'll soon find out," the mother had said. It was a struggle to keep up and there were so many puddles that got in the way. The suitcase had become heavier and bumped against her legs.

The Red Cross lady suddenly turned through an archway. The torch shone on big, open metal gates like the ones at school. She wondered if she would ever see her school again.

She wanted to go home and be warm by the fire. Perhaps someone would give her cocoa and a biscuit when they got to the hostel. Was that a sort of hotel? She had been in a hotel once at her auntie's wedding. The lavatory had been lovely, so pretty, with flowers. She had thrown little bits of coloured paper at her auntie and new uncle. The motor car her new uncle took auntie off in had things tied on the back and something written on a big notice in the window. When the tins and things clattered out from under the car she thought the uncle would stop and take them off but he laughed and waved and kept going.

The Red Cross lady stopped in front of a big door and looked round from under her hat. "Here we are," she said. "Make haste inside. We must na' let out the light!" Lucy had listened to her voice while they were at the train station. It sounded different, not like granny or great-aunt Lilian back in Sussex.

The lady had called her baby brother 'the bairn'. "Shall I take the bairn?" she had said. But her baby brother had started to cry and had hung onto her mother's collar.

"He's upset, I'll carry him," her mother had said. So the Red Cross lady had switched on her torch and taken the suitcase, smiling at Lucy as they walked out onto the wet, dark street.

They had walked a long way, past shops and two beer houses. She knew they were beer houses. They had the smell that great-uncle John had when he came back at dinner time on Sundays. He was always jolly then and wasn't tired out like on weekdays when he worked on the farm with the big horses.

Suddenly they were inside and it was just like school,

all the mothers with their children and babies who were crying. She wondered which ones were the teachers and if the mothers would be leaving. But there were beds here. Little beds, with grey blankets. No white sheets. The light bulbs hanging from their long wires had no shades.

She wondered if she would have to get into her pyjamas in front of all those people.

"These are yours," the lady said, pointing to two beds. They had curvy pipes instead of legs like at home. "There's lavatories and basins there, and a fountain," the lady said, pointing to a green door. "I'll be back in the morn."

Lucy noticed some people had cups. Was it cocoa? There were other ladies, dressed like the Red Cross lady, at a table with a big shiny urn. She knew it was called an urn because there had been one at the wedding. Her new uncle had been called Urn too, which she thought was funny.

"Mum," she called across to the other bed where her mother was unclipping the big case and getting out the brown wash-bag. "Mum, I'm thirsty."

"In a minute," her mother said. "We'll go and find the fountain." Water! She didn't want cold water.

"Mum!" She pointed towards the table where she could see some mothers and even children getting something in white cups. She remembered the day in her school at dinner time when her steaming cup of Oxo, that she always had with her sandwich, had tipped and spilled all over her legs. Teacher had rushed over to help her. She had sat on the sick bed at the side of the classroom with her skirt pulled right up and the tops of her legs covered in cool white paste. She had still been able to do the lesson though.

Her mother had put the wash-bag and small towel on the bed.

"I'll see what I can get."

"Cocoa," Lucy called. "I really want some cocoa." Cocoa would make her feel better, make her tummy stop hurting. She was very hungry.

All she had at dinner time was a jam sandwich – she didn't like cheese. Auntie had put it in her pocket just before the taxi had arrived to take them to the station to begin their journey to Canada where there wasn't any war or any ack-ack guns shooting at the droning doodlebugs with the red light. If that light went out, her mother had said, the thing would fall straight down and explode.

Her mother had been very afraid of the doodlebugs and had sometimes stood at the window in Lucy's bedroom as one flew over the trees and the soldiers' camp across the road.

Lucy would wake to hear her mother making moaning noises and would see the shadows moving on the wall.

That was because the searchlight that the soldiers kept hidden under a green cover had come on.

The doodlebug would be caught in the bright white light and the clattering of the gun would start. It shot hundreds of silvery bullets straight up the beam of light. Then the thing would go into a cloud. The gun would stop and the searchlight would try to find it again but it would have gone over the house and on towards London.

One hot night when the window was wide open, the gun had stopped. Then she heard a swishing, whistling noise like a big wind and her mother had flopped straight down on Lucy, squashing her into the bed and nearly stopping her breath. There had been a big boom that had made the room shake and the jug in the basin on the washstand had rattled. Her mother rushed to the window and looked up the road. Lucy's friend Jennifer lived in the next house a long way up the road. "No, it's alright. It must have landed further up," her mother had said. "It's alright now, go back to sleep."

Lucy had wondered why the soldiers had made a camp right there, just after she and her mother came to Sussex to live with great-auntie and uncle to "get away from the bombs". There were lots of other places they could have made a camp where it wouldn't have been seen by the German planes.

It was more frightening in great-auntie's house than before. But then she remembered that the siren hardly ever came on at her new school so she didn't need to keep going into a shelter with a gas mask.

The siren hadn't even sounded when the boys' school, that was on the way home, got bombed. It had been bombed in the afternoon when all the boys were there. All except Tom, the postlady's boy who lived just along the road, because he was at his woodworking class. Lucy remembered standing on the pavement with her mother and a lot of other mothers and fathers as the big black cars with flowers went past ever so slowly to the cemetery. People were crying, even some men.

She didn't know then that boys were in the boxes in those cars. She didn't know then that boys could die, just be gone forever in a box. She thought that only people like grannies and granddads died and went to heaven.

She hoped auntie Lil and uncle John wouldn't die while she was in Canada and she really hoped too that the soldiers wouldn't move camp before she came back because there might be another Christmas party there. She had put the doll that she had got for a present into the tin trunk with all the clothes that had been sent on before. She hoped it wouldn't get lost.

Friendship
By Valerie Nye

The boy trailed slowly down the street, clicking his fingers to a small brown dog at his heels. His head was bent and he was speaking softly to the animal as it jumped up at him.

As they neared the corner house the boy's steps dragged. Glancing at the windows, he saw a slight movement of the curtains.

With a sigh he opened the gate a little and squeezed in, shutting it quickly behind him to keep the dog out. He leaned over the top, looked into the deep brown eyes lifted up to his and whispered, "Go away fellow, go back. I'll see you later."

The dog whined and pawed at the wooden gate. The boy sensed the front door opening. He banged the top of the gate with his fist. "Go away!" he shouted and turned towards the house.

His aunt said nothing as he slipped past her. She lifted a stone and hurled it at the gate. The startled dog set off down the road to the sound of the front door being slammed shut.

In the kitchen the aunt gave him his tea – and her views on mangy strays carrying who-knows-what diseases. "If I see him again I'll do more than throw stones!" she threatened.

The boy knew that 'strays' meant him as well as the dog. She had reluctantly agreed to take him in when his parents had died. He was housed and fed and had no place to expect more than that. The dog was his only source of comfort, his only experience now of love and affection.

After tea he withdrew silently to his bedroom and watched for the dog to reappear, as he knew he would. He came out of the woods on the far side of the house. He skirted the hedge, forced his way through a hole then took up position squatting in the shadows.

The boy slipped out onto the landing. There was no sound. His aunt must have gone out.

Reassured by the darkness he crept into the kitchen. His scalp prickled as the door creaked but the noise brought the dog running. The boy picked him up and rubbed his face in the rough brown fur, murmuring idiotic things into his floppy ears.

The aunt's voice boomed out. He was blinking in the sudden glare of the kitchen light. The cowering dog was snatched from his arms. He saw a raised poker and the dog howled just once before an awful silence. He covered his ears but the dog moaned on in his mind.

Shut away in his bedroom later he heard her walking along the path to the woods. He ran to the window and saw her, dragging the pathetic little body by its hind legs.

When she came back her hands were empty. The boy knew what he must do. The next morning before she came downstairs he hid an old knife in his satchel. And when he returned from school it was as if the dog was still beside him.

He opened the gate a little and squeezed in, shutting it quickly behind him.

His aunt saw him but ignored his childish pretence, perhaps in an attempt to settle an uneasy conscience. But as the days passed and he maintained the same routine, the aunt began to believe she could see the dog behind him. Once, waking in the night, she heard the clicking of the dog's nails on the stairs.

Finally she went to the woods again and the boy watched her with a smile on his face.

When she ran into his room he was still smiling, stroking the sightless skull of the dog. From its bony jaws a warm red tongue came out to lick his fingers.

The Seagull
By Michael Downes

It is cold and windy when he steps out of the car that morning and makes his way down to the shore. His face catches the full brunt of the sea wind, his hair flying wildly.

He trudges along the wet sand out of reach of the foaming incoming tide, his hands deep in the pockets of the anorak. The long stretch of strand is deserted but he has not come down here to enjoy the view. He is here to collect his thoughts.

It was on this beach he told her he had never met anyone like her, he was hopelessly in love. She was more cautious but allowed him into her heart. She reminded him on many occasions where it would all lead.

She asked if he regretted ever meeting her that day. He had been cruising the neighbourhood in the patrol car when he came upon a confrontation on the kerb.

An old Morris sedan had run into the backside of a Ford Customline. Two young bucks were screaming abuse at a dark-haired Asian woman. He parked and crossed the street. The young men shouted at him, "Look what this fucken Chinese bitch has gone and done!"

She turned to face him. That was when he noticed how lovely she looked, no fear or anger, just calm and resolute. Unlike these two hotheads.

When he said it looked like they had driven their Morris into the back end of the Customline, it made them more mad.

"You gunna take her side?" one of them yelled. "I bet she doesn't even 'ave a license to drive the fucken thing. Bet she shouldn't even be in the country."

He checked all their licenses, then he checked the damage to both vehicles.

"Take this up with your insurance companies. You got insurance?" he asked the young men.

They didn't answer.

"No insurance eh? Too bad."

He made them hand over their details to her. They swore and called her names. He reminded them they were one step away from the cop shop if they didn't shut it.

They roared off in a cloud of smoke. He told her he would follow her just in case the two guys were still around. She thanked him. Then she told him she was Japanese, not Chinese. She worked for the Japanese Consulate as an interpreter.

"I've never met a Japanese woman before," he told her. "I suppose there's not many of your kind here in Sydney is there?"

He realised his words could be misconstrued, and he made a feeble attempt to address it. She stopped him and smiled. Her look, her voice, her smile, it captivated him.

"What is your name?" she asked.

"Jack. Jack Curry. I'm stationed at Bondi Junction if you ever. . ." He shrugged his shoulders. "What's your name? Hang on I already know that. Ryoko, isn't it?"

She laughed. "Yes! And you pronounced it correctly too."

He laughed with her. She was even prettier when she laughed.

"Well I'd better follow you just in case those two are hanging about. Do you live around here?"

"Bondi Junction."

"Oh, good. . . good."

He didn't want to leave. She stood there smiling as if she didn't want him to.

He followed her to the apartment building where she lived. He watched as she climbed the steps to the entrance where she turned and waved.

Japanese. He would never have thought that. And he would keep this to himself. The war in the Pacific had ended ten years ago but the scars of the conflict were still fresh. Nothing had been forgotten, nothing forgiven.

All that week he would pass by the apartments in the hope he might see her. He never did. And then one day out of the blue the desk sergeant told him that a large box of chocolates had been dropped off in his name by a very pretty Asian girl. After that he saw her almost every day.

Finally he told his parents that he was dating a Japanese girl. The fallout was horrendous. His father refused to speak to him and his cousins kept their distance. His family had lost three uncles to the Japanese – one as a prisoner of war, the other two in the jungles of New Guinea. He understood their hatred and at the same time hated them for their bigotry. He explained all of this to her.

It was no different in her family, she said. Her father lost his life in Burma, and all his brothers at various stages of the war. She told him every family in Japan had lost a loved one.

Many times he thought about breaking up with her, but every time he saw her, held her, made love to her, he knew he couldn't. And when he wasn't with her the thought of walking away and never seeing her again crept back. It tore at him like nothing he'd ever experienced before, and she knew it.

"This will end one day. . . you know that, don't you?" Those were her words only days before she vanished. He still didn't see it coming.

The part that hurt the most was when he went to her apartment to find it deserted.

He got no help from the Japanese Consulate. They told him she had returned to Japan. Nothing more than that. Security was called and he was escorted off the premises.

With nothing but her name he had virtually no way of finding her. He searched her apartment for any lead, a scrap of paper, even a name. Nothing.

His close friends told him what he didn't want to hear. But of course he dismissed their comments, refused to believe that she had planned all of this.

He moped in self pity for months. He did not know what to do and he did not care. He had not reported for duty for nearly a week now.

Cries from a flock of seagulls hovering against the wind catch his attention. As he approaches he notices one is dead on the sand.

He touches its white breast. It's soft, even warm. Why should it find its last resting place on this lonely beach?

Above him the gulls' cries are growing louder until at last they move off along the shoreline.

This bird was probably alive and well this morning. Now it lies here, it will never again fly with its own kind or feel the sea wind against its wings.

He remembers a quote from some school text, 'I never saw a wild thing sorry for itself'.

He thought of her, her words that this would end one day. He looked at his watch: 9.30. He turned and hurried back to the car. His shift had already started.

The Game
By Celia Berggreen

The gravel always made such a satisfying, crunching sound. When Lizzie jumped out of the back door she sent tiny stones scattering and skidding against the wall.

Today she had her hula hoop with her. She liked to hold it round her waist and when no-one was watching she would make furtive moves and wiggles to make the hoop spin round. It still fell down round her feet though.

Mummy had said she was busy today. It seemed to involve lying on the sofa with her eyes closed, so perhaps she was having very busy thoughts. Lizzie tried standing still and closing her eyes, but she couldn't stop her feet scrunching and rolling the little pebbles underfoot. And no thoughts of any importance seemed to arrive. She decided her mind must be busy enough already and opened her eyes again to find Mr Carmichael from next door smiling across at her.

The Carmichael's front door was at the side of the house and it was always perfectly gleaming. Mr Carmichael had the polish and duster in his hand. He was just starting on the big brass door knocker.

"And a very merry morning to you, Miss Lizzie!"

Mr Carmichael was always saying funny things like that to her. It made Lizzie laugh. Then he would open his eyes very wide in astonishment. "And what, pray, do you find so amusing?" He was teasing, she knew he was. She decided a long time ago that he wished he had a little girl too, instead of his two much older sons.

Alan and Peter Carmichael went to the Boys' Independent school in the next village.

"Terribly bright," Lizzie's mother was fond of telling her friends. "Terribly bright boys."

Lizzie often thought she wouldn't want to be terribly bright if it meant your face flaming scarlet like Alan Carmichael's did whenever he saw Lizzie's older sister Clare.

And she didn't understand why being so clever meant you talked in that odd, abrupt way that Peter Carmichael did, the words shooting and spurting out of his mouth as if they were being fired by a rather jerky pop gun. If he met them in the village street he would scurry past with his head down, a staccato "Good morning!" under his breath. Lizzie had never seen Peter laugh or even smile much. He was so serious. Not at all like his father.

She couldn't imagine Mr Carmichael ever finding pennies behind Peter's ear. He often found them behind Lizzie's, pennies that she never remembered putting there – why would she have? Often he let her keep them too.

Mrs Carmichael was as wide and unkempt as her husband was narrow and neat. Lizzie caught a glimpse of her now, over the side wall, in the Carmichael's back garden. She was hanging out the washing, a cigarette dangling limply from the corner of her mouth. Today she was wearing a baggy cardigan, fastened with an enormous safety pin, over a droopy yellowing blouse. An unevenly-hemmed skirt was straining to fit over her increasingly-large waist.

Sometimes the washing would stay out there for two or three days, the cause of much tutting from Lizzie's mother. Mrs Carmichael was quite friendly to Lizzie but in a terse, brisk way, quite different from her husband.

Today Mr Carmichael called out, "And what might we be doing today?"

"I'm practising, Mr Carmichael," Lizzie explained, concentrating hard on keeping her hoop above her tummy. Once it started to tip down, all was lost. You just had to start again.

"For the circus perhaps?"

Lizzie giggled. "I bet you can't guess today. I bet you can't guess without looking!"

It was a favourite game.

Mr Carmichael changed his twinkly face for a rather solemn one. He put down the polish and duster, and wagged his finger at Lizzie. "Now, little Miss, am I ever wrong?"

He turned round with his back to her, so that he was facing his big, lustrous black door. The whole of the top half of the door was patterned with small panes of glass, sparkling and shining like the hard glossy mints Lizzie's father enjoyed after supper.

"Now!" Lizzie shouted in excitement. "What am I doing now?"

"Well now." There was a long considering silence. "Well now, would you by any chance be standing on one foot?"

Lizzie wobbled. "Yes! Yes! You're right! And what now?"

"Hmm. Quite a tricky one. Hands on your head?"

"How do you know? How can you guess? What about now?"

"Easy-peasy. Waving. Who are you waving at, little Miss Lizzie?"

"You! You! I'm waving at you of course! Tell me! Tell me how you know!"

Mr Carmichael turned round to face her again. Behind him the tiny panes of glass winked and glinted in the early afternoon sun.

"Eyes in the back of my head, little Lizzie. Eyes in the back of my head."

The Moth
By Keith Windsor

I'm not a wimp. I'm a criminal barrister, top dog in chambers. I've managed to contend with every gross human insanity. I have never shirked.

But, there is one thing that always freaks me out. I've suffered from it all my life. I don't know, perhaps it was something that happened in the pram.

I have a phobia with moths. Not any little moth, but the large moth. Those sinister grey-brown, peculiar, brindled moths.

I was coming home on an unusually crowded train in August. Ten minutes to my station, I gathered my things together and happened to glance up. There it was. At rest with its wings outstretched. Enormous.

I felt my whole consciousness sink from my being, but I couldn't take my eyes from it. It was above the aisle where I had to exit.

Suddenly it fluttered down on to the back of the seat next to me. I froze. My eyes wide staring at my nemesis, I began to shake uncontrollably.

I felt a reassuring hand on my knee and a man gently but firmly told me to take deep breaths, and that I would be alright.

"It's only a moth, it can't hurt you." As he took it in his hand he said, "I'll release him into the air at the next station. Carry on with the deep breaths, you're doing well. What's your name, love?"

"Liz," I replied meekly.

"My name's Alan. I'm a paramedic. Now this little fellow won't cause you any harm Liz, remember that. You're doing well."

I followed him off the train at a distance and watched as he released it into some bushes. He saw me standing there and guided me to a seat. I couldn't help looking at his hand, but it was empty.

"Are you okay to travel home now Liz?"

"Thanks, I'm much better."

"You look better. Your colour has returned."

I found my car in the multi-storey. The day was turning into one of those rare warm summer evenings and I was looking forward to having a drink on the terrace before supper.

As I rounded the corner by the Dyke, I reached up to

take the sun visor down. Something large and brindled flew into my face.

I remember seeing the lorry, too late.

"What's your name, love?"

"Liz," I mumbled.

"Can we call you Liz? You're going to be alright, we'll get you to hospital. My name is Alan. Just stay with me Liz, listen to me Liz, stay with me."

All Sides of the Story
By Anne Whitehead

Martha worried about her daughter, and was exhausted by the time she'd seen Florence through a turbulent and distressing adolescence. Her husband Frank simply prayed for a miracle to keep Florence in line. And along it came. Dave, one in a long stream of brief relationships, stuck around.

They were delighted with Dave, saw how he patiently coaxed Florence out of her black moods, and for a while they thought she was ready to move on. She wasn't, she just played around behind his back. They worried about what would happen if he found out but said nothing, praying it would all come out right in the end. Dave was their best hope.

Florence and Dave married and everyone got on with their lives. Dave had a steady job and Florence undertook a series of temporary jobs in between producing three daughters in five years.

By then it was clear that Florence was incapable of providing any stability for them, being erratic at best and unhinged at worst.

F   My parents' assumption that I would want what they had really irritated me. From an early age I did all I could to test their limits – smoking, drinking, obvious promiscuity – but nothing rocked them. I wanted to leave home when school ended but couldn't afford it. I had loads of jobs but every single one of them was ruined by colleagues who obviously hated me and I never made friends.

Then I went into town one Friday night with colleagues from the latest job. I'd only been there a week and joined them in their monthly blow-out. They never invited me again so it was a good job I met Dave that night. I got hammered and he, all chivalry, called a cab and delivered me home. The next morning I found a slip of paper in my bag and had a vague recollection of asking one of his group where they worked and shakily writing it down.

On Monday I rang him at work, telling him I'd mislaid my keys, asked if he had them. There were in my bag but he wouldn't have known that as Dad had answered the door that night. I hinted that I'd had a bit of trauma at work which is why I'd got so drunk. I thought that would flick his knight-in-shining-armour switch. It did and we arranged to meet again.

D   I met Florence after work one Friday night. I didn't usually go out drinking but it was Jim's birthday and all were invited to the club. I'm pretty shy but a lively girl came over, threw her arm around my shoulder and insisted on a dance. She was obviously drunk but I didn't want to embarrass her by refusing so off we went. An hour later she was clinging to me like a limpet, sobbing that her life was rubbish. I thought I'd better see her home.

We met up the next weekend and she was apologetic about her behaviour that night and I took her previous brashness as a cover for vulnerability. She told me that she'd been through quite a lot, and it made me feel important, like I'd helped someone in their hour of need. That's how I fell for her.

F   I made Dave wait a while before I slept with him and he was patient and very respectful. From then on keeping him onside was easy. When I went too far I'd give him the 'I hate myself for being difficult routine' and he just caved in.

Nearly a year in, when I told him I was pregnant, he

was shocked – hadn't I taken my pill? Of course, I said, but that last stomach upset, being sick must have caused it to be ineffective. He believed it. Next thing he's proposing and I'm crying and saying yes. Tears of relief but he didn't need to know that.

It was a small wedding. We hadn't seen much of his parents, I'd made sure of that. They arrived for the Registry Office ceremony, drove home immediately after and were killed in a crash on the motorway. Not their fault, the lorry driver was fatigued, had lost control. An ambulance chaser came along, got us a nice compensation package from the negligent firm and we were set up to start our new life together. All very satisfactory.

Dave grieved. I showered him with sympathy for a couple of weeks then suggested we needed to concentrate on the future. Shame our children would never know his parents but what could we do?

D   It was a shock, losing Mum and Dad like that. With Florence around I hadn't gone home much, and felt that I'd neglected them. Florence had been wonderful after the crash, and helped me see that we had to look to the future.

This turned out to be Jasmine, Ruby and baby Sita, who was named during Florence's temporary preoccupation with all things Eastern. I was grateful she hadn't been born during her mother's dalliance with the arty set, one of whom had called her son Pablo. Pablo Wilkins. That poor lad would go through hell at the local comprehensive.

F I thought of our daughters as cement, holding Dave fast to me. Shortly after Sita was born I went off to London with a new man I'd met in a bar, but it turned sour. I'd told him I had a violent husband, felt scared and all the rest, and moved to London with him, but he soon threw me out. Said he'd felt sorry for me having such a terrible marriage but I was too unstable.

D I was appalled when Florence left for London when Sita was only six months old. Martha came to stay and Frank joined us at weekends. I don't know what I'd have done without them.

Life became very peaceful. Jasmine chatted away instead of being afraid of irritating Florence, and Ruby loved to paint which had been banned as too messy. Sita settled down, slept through the night, accepted and enjoyed all her food.

Everything changed when Florence came back. I contacted a solicitor, who said that if I tried for custody I'd lose. Courts always sided with the mother. She had me over a barrel.

F I was disappointed to find it was all happy families when I returned from London, but managed to get rid of Martha pretty sharpish. Off she stumbled, telling me I needed to be more responsible blah blah. Dave just got on with it. If we parted and he tried for custody, he'd lose. I was their mother. I wondered what he'd do if he realised that one of those precious girls wasn't his.

Life ground on. I carried on clubbing, the release in the dancing and the excitement of new men keeping me going. Being at home was hell. I've never felt so sorry for myself.

D One Saturday morning Florence was out and I was at home with the girls playing round the kitchen table. It was a wet, murky day and as I put the light on they all looked up at me and my heart turned over. When she was born we'd called Sita our little changeling, but she now really looked nothing like Jasmine or Ruby, who both had my colouring and the slightly wonky nose bequeathed by my parents. I got out our family photos.

M One rainy Saturday we went round, knowing that Florence would be out. They were playing with family photographs and at first glance it looked lovely, until we noticed the look on Dave's face.

Frank and I went to take a look and the realisation hit

us hard. We left soon after, telling the girls we had to get back before dark, too shocked to stay.

F   I managed to get away one Saturday, telling Dave I was going shopping. I was late back and thought Dave was annoyed as he hardly spoke for a couple of days. Then the girls told me about the photo game, and I realised he knew. So what?

M   My heart was so sore I thought it would snap. The pain Florence had caused played on my mind relentlessly. Then one day I woke up filled with an unbearable mixture of rage and hurt. I told Frank I was going shopping but instead drove to their house, knowing that Dave would be at work and the girls at school.

She was still in her dressing gown, drinking coffee and watching TV, and looked bored while she listened to me ranting. Hey, she said, at last. Something's finally cracked you.

Her callousness made me sick. I turned and picked up the heavy vase that stood on the mantelpiece and with indescribable pain in my heart I brought it down on my daughter's head.

Cedar Heights
By Clive Boothman

Beyond the chimes of Sunday bells, the view from the lounge windows floats away to where the sun straddles the hills. In Cedar Heights, the carers have been helping people into armchairs.

My eyes wander over to Rommy and I know him well enough to guess that the distant look in his eyes means he's thinking of the coming weekend's mountain biking. He's broad-shouldered which helps him look after the frail people with dementia who live here.

To my left a conversation has started.

"No Dad. You were alright till you were eighty."

"So how old am I now?"

"You're eleven by eight." Did a twinkle of mischief light up Tom's face?

"That's eighty eight isn't it?" John smiles.

"That's right."

"And when did I start with this?"

"It started when you were eighty but you had a fall last year and it's got worse since."

From beyond the chairs, at the opposite side of the lounge, a woman's voice, one used to getting what its owner wants. "I can't stay here any longer. . ."

It's only been a few minutes since breakfast and at first there's silence. Then, from the other side of the glass panelled doors, "Where do you want to be, Mary?" Will lopes in, pushing a wooden medicine trolley.

"Somewhere more comfortable."

"I'll fetch some cushions."

"I'd rather be in my room."

"Will they find a cure?" John resumes.

"Maybe," Tom replies. "They're still looking."

"I hope so. I don't want you to get it."

"Neither do I, Dad."

Television has drawn some people into its news and gossip but has turned others off, into the day's long doze.

Sooner than you'd imagine, it's time for tea and the guests are brought to the tables. They're quietly expectant apart from Sue who's sitting upright, eyes peering towards those at her table. Yesterday she'd been either asleep or staring with streaming, red-veined eyes. Now it's a more excited Sue who is rapping the wood with a metal spoon.

Then I notice the drumming is in rhythm with the light that has started to flicker, sending shadows of the lampshade up and down the walls. Some of the guests have started to follow the patterns with their eyes.

"Are you all right, Sue?" Grace inquires. "You're making a lot of noise."

Joy, too, has gone over and is bending, at eye level with Sue. "Oh, Will," she calls. "There is something wrong with this light."

There's a gasp of breath from the other guests who realise that Sue is ignoring the carers and her noise is getting louder. She's showing no signs of stopping.

"What's that?" Sue exclaims. "Look, it's the light."

Soon she's banging out another rhythm on the table. "Light, more light!" she shouts as the light carries on wobbling.

When next I look up, there are four or five carers in the room and the Manager is approaching Sue who's still in a trance.

There's a lull as the spoon rests and a conversation resumes in the background.

"Where am I?" John asks, in the expectant silence created by Will rummaging amongst the bulb packages.

"You're in Cedar Heights, Dad," Tom replies. "Best place for you."

"You're very kind," John grins.

And just as suddenly as it stopped, the spoon starts banging again and again. Sue's look is even more determined. "More light, more light!" she shouts as her teatime companions stare on.

And now I remember what people have said about Sue – she used to be the restaurant manager in a local hotel.

"Come on all of you, all hands to the pumps! And fix that light will you? How can we serve food when you're all just sitting around?" she's ranting, her eyes raking in everyone, carers and guests.

"Ooh, what's happening to her?" one of the women exclaims.

"I'm the only one round here who can hold down a proper job. The rest of you. . ."

"Stop that noise will you?" John growls.

I see Tom placing his hand on John's wrist. "Don't get yourself excited, Dad."

Then things begin to happen. "Room 19," is all the Manager says as she nods to Rommy, Joy and Grace.

Rommy swivels a wheelchair while the others whisper into Sue's ears, touch her arms and ease her from the chair. She gazes and then complies. As she's manoeuvred away, she looks up at the bulb Will has taken from its shade. Now the only light in the lounge is the television.

Sue is already through the door and is booming to the empty corridor: "Light, more light. . . Endless streams. . . Light, more light! "

I remember that as she's led to Room 19 she'll pass the sign on the wall:

If you've met one person with dementia you've met
one person with dementia.

Girl in Shorts
By Yvonne Ayres

A dark grey light creeps around the edges of my
bedroom curtains and the dawn chorus grows steadily
noisier as the sun rises. In the ghostly half-light I can
see the outline of the dress hanging up in its clear
plastic cover. Reluctantly I throw back the duvet and
tiptoe across the carpet. Lifting the bottom corner
of the plastic I risk a quick, tentative touch of the
material. It feels so different to my favourite denim
shorts. I don't do dresses, so I don't know what Mum
was thinking when she bought it. I suppose she
wants me to wear it tonight. But I haven't even tried
it on, because I'm not wearing it or going to the party,
whatever anyone says. I'm staying home with Dougal.

Opening the curtains I watch the pale sun playing
hide 'n seek with the grey clouds moving slowly across
the sky. Much as I'd like to I can't ignore the day. I have

to follow my normal routine. I struggle to cope with anything different. Another reason I can't go to the party, social events are not something I normally do. Hearing signs of movement from my big sister's room I head to the bathroom for a shower before she gets up. Jamie takes forever to have a shower so I always have to jump in first. Leaving the bathroom with dripping hair and remembering that my hairdryer's busted, I march straight into Jamie's room.

"Can I borrow your hairdryer?"

"No, go away. It's the middle of the night," she shouts and pulls the duvet over her head.

"Please." Someone touches my shoulder. I spin round angrily. It's Dad standing behind me in his pjs. He knows I don't like any physical contact, or he should do by now, after all I'll be fifteen next month. Dad quickly drops his hand, but not before he gives me that look. I don't really understand what the look means, but he's not smiling.

"Why don't you just get dressed, love? Leave your hair for now. It is a bit early for a Saturday." I glare at him. My hair takes ages to dry without a hairdryer. I move towards the chest of drawers where I know Jamie keeps it, but there isn't room for me to get past Dad without touching him. Frustrated I try another fierce glare while battling the instinctive urge to lash out.

"Get Out Of My Room," screams Jamie loud enough to wake the whole street.

"You're up and showered nice and early this morning. Want to use my hairdryer?" I hadn't heard Mum get up. I'd rather use Jamie's dryer but I suppose Mum's old one will have to do.

Hair finally dry, I get dressed in my usual shorts and tee-shirt and go in search of Dougal. He's waiting by the back door, lead in his mouth, eager for our morning walk.

I wasn't sure about Dougal at first, all that jumping up and licking stuff freaked me out. But I'm used to having him around now. He's my only friend, apart from Marta who lives miles away so I only see her at school. She hasn't been in this country long so doesn't talk much because she's still learning the language. But that suits me. I don't talk much either so we get on great. Mum and Dad invited Marta to the party and for a sleepover, but she's already promised to babysit her cousins so can't come. I'm certainly not going to the party without her.

Straight after breakfast Mum and Dad go to the village hall to let the caterers in. Jamie's still in bed so it's just Dougal and me again, which is cool. My phone pings with a text from Marta, 'Babys sick. Can come to party.' My first thought is great, closely followed by a sinking feeling. Does this mean I'll have to go to the party? Before I can reply to Marta, Jamie appears asking me who the text is from. I just shrug and go to my room.

The hated dress is still hanging there. Going to the party wouldn't be quite so bad if I could go in my shorts. I stare at the dress, willing it to disappear. Lifting it down I snatch it from the hanger and throw it onto my bed in a tangle of flimsy fabric and plastic.

"Careful. It'll get creased." I turn round and there's Jamie at my half-open door, spying on me again. I feel the heat of rage rising. I haven't felt this angry in a long while, not since the last time I got told off at school for wearing my shorts instead of the uniform skirt. Then I'd lashed out at everyone, kicking and screaming. That was before I'd been diagnosed as being on the autistic spectrum and started getting some help. I'm still learning how to control my temper. Jamie strolls in and looks at the price tag still attached to the dress.

"You haven't even bothered to try this on yet have you?" I daren't even look at her let alone reply. My nails dig painfully into the palms of my hands as I struggle to stay calm. "It wouldn't hurt you to make an effort just this once for Mum and Dad would it? It's their silver wedding anniversary." She unwraps the dress from its plastic cover and holds it up, waiting for me to take it and try it on. It's too much. I drop my phone, rush out of the door and down the stairs.

Grabbing Dougal's lead I head outside, the dog at my heels. Once in the wood at the end of our road I let out a scream and kick at anything within reach. Dougal sits patiently at my side, it's as if he understands what I'm going through. As soon as I feel calmer I start to walk. Dougal trots along looking up at me every so often as if to check I'm okay. That's when my tears start. He licks my face as I squat down beside him.

"You okay?" It's Jamie. I look up at her chin avoiding eye contact. "How come you can let a dog lick you, but can't tolerate even a touch from anyone else?" she asks. I don't know the answer to that, any more than I know why I can only bear to wear shorts all the time even on cold winter days when my knees are numb. "Oh come on, you oddball. Mum and Dad will wonder where we are."

The village hall looks so different. There's fairy lights everywhere and lots of those battery tea-light things that flicker and glow. The music's a bit dodgy, but all the oldies are jigging about to it, including Mum and Dad. Jamie's standing with a crowd of her mates, centre of attention as usual. Marta and I are sitting in the corner watching everyone. She enjoys just people watching and that's okay by me. It's not been too bad especially as Dougal's here. I've managed to avoid the bloke going around taking photos, until Jamie comes up and tells me

I'm needed for a family picture. I'm just about to refuse when I feel Dougal's rough tongue licking my hand.

I stand between Mum and Jamie in the hated dress and smile obediently. I even managed not to flinch when Dad brushed past me at the end of the evening. I felt I owed him one, after all it was Dad who suggested that Dougal should come to the party. But tomorrow I'll be wearing my beloved shorts.

Midsummer Magic
By Linda Preston

I lay on my bed willing my eyes to close but they would not. I put the pillow over my face but it got too hot. The light was streaming in the bedroom window through curtains too thin, and too small to meet in the middle. I could hear the radio downstairs. Mum and Dad were laughing.

I got up and opened the window to catch a breeze, and a chance to see what was going on in the street. I could hear drums, and a fiddle. Out of sight, but in the direction of the old priory ruins. Was it a party?

They wouldn't check my room. Especially if it was quiet. They wouldn't know if I popped out for just an hour to see the party. I dressed and climbed out onto the roof of our privy to reach the wall overhung with branches from the ash tree. Holding on to the leafy branches, I balanced along the wall to the end where it was easier to jump to the ground. I cut round the backs to avoid the window of our front room where I might be spotted.

At the end of our road, by the side of the ruins, was the Mount. A perfect hump of grass, higher than the houses but not as high as the castle in town. I often played on it and tried to guess how it got there. Could it be an ancient lookout for invaders? A rubbish heap from building a salt pan? And when was the spiral path to the top made?

I followed the sound to the Mount. At the top, a space about a quarter the size of a football pitch, there were a dozen people in fancy dress, a bit like the Morris Men you see at Easter. A woman in white was dancing with long ribbons curling through the air, while a fiddler and drummer played. Girls were making crowns from the flowers on the slopes. An old man with long curly hair and a black fingertip jacket held a gnarled wooden stick and pointed to the distant beacon.

"The sun will rise at four thirty." He looked around at everyone and nodded sagely.

I sat on the grass, sweet smelling and soft. I felt at home amongst them, accepted without question. They shared a jug of juice and herby flapjacks. I did a jumping, kicking dance to the rhythm of the drum and everyone clapped. They were waiting for the sun and I wanted to stay and see it rise too. At four thirty Mum and Dad would be sound asleep, and not have any idea if I was in bed or not. If my empty sheets had already been discovered I might as well be hanged for a sheep as a lamb.

As the time got close to sunrise we were all very quiet and peering in the same direction. The old man said some words, and looked at the sky.

"Let's pray for a clear view." We all looked up at the broken cloud cover and I crossed my fingers on both hands.

In the silence and the tension on that hilltop, I swear I held my breath for ages. Then the sky glowed a golden haze. Was that it? Where was the ball of fire we were watching for. Then the rim of the sun sneaked over the horizon. The musicians played a quickening rhythm and we cheered and threw our arms in the air. The leader looked upwards and recited something in strange words. Was it a prayer?

The people held hands in a circle drawing me into the chain, and we walked round three times, then the leader let go of one hand and led the chain down the spiral pathway to the bottom of the Mount. It was done and everyone disappeared in different directions.

I ran back up the road, but I couldn't climb up to my bedroom window. It was not like jumping down. I sat on the back step and dreamily pictured the night.

I tried to recite the words of the sunrise prayer and then found my legs quiver with strength I never had before. With one bound I was up to the windowsill of my room and able to climb through undetected.

I still couldn't sleep, but Mum found me under the sheets, with eyes closed tight at eight o'clock.

A Sound Journey
By Harriet Townsend

As the sun sets, the women crowd at the bars of the cell window, mosquitoes drone round their sweating faces, but they crane to listen to the solitary drummer who sits on the beach far, far below.

The beat drifts up on the sea breeze into the fortress and for a few moments the crush of bodies, the stench of boredom, the heat, fade with the drum-beats into the dwindling light.

The prisoners are barefoot, even the western girls, their shoes removed to avoid their possible use as weapons in the frequent savage fights. They wear knee-length shifts of unbleached calico, which rub the open sores and insect bites.

From the window, the drummer is an insect-like black shape, just visible under the palms. The white breakers crash on the darkening sand.

In the bay, a tourist boat is returning to the jetty. As always at this time, the voice of the guide cuts across the gentle beat and floats up to the listeners at the window.

"And finally, ladies and gentlemen, on the headland, you can see our oldest prison, built by the Portuguese. We put some very naughty girls in there. . ."

Then the boat, a white dot on the water, turns and moors. The tourists, bleary with sun and sea, climb out onto the tiny wooden jetty and disappear among the shadowy palm trees fringing the path to the village.

The drumming stops.

A shout, and the women turn and form a jostling line to pick up the round metal tali dishes, ready for the evening vegetable curry and rice.

A pale face in the crowd, Helen catches her reflection in the surface of her dish. *Who is this?* – the lank unwashed hair, sallow skin and the dull eyes that look back at her.

A new girl, Thai perhaps, elbows her and the dish clatters to the floor. "Ferengi. . . parcel. . . food from England. . . America. . . I have friends."

Her face is too close and the spray of spittle, a familiar acrid reek, lingers.

"Piss off. I get nothing now. Even the bloody Consul's forgotten me. He hasn't been for weeks."

Helen breaks away from the shuffling queue, her

stomach queasy as usual. Hunger is preferable to a wretched night stumbling over sleeping women to the stinking hole in the corner. She moves back to the bars, feeling a faint coolness lift her hair.

It is dark now, except for a line of green on the horizon – a single lamp on a bobbing fishing boat.

Silence until the drummer returns in the dusk tomorrow night.

A Brief Encounter
By Ian Riddle

I first met her – this girl destined to become either the love of my life or the bane of it, depending on perspective – just off the motorway, at the shopping centre on the road that joins the towns of Rheims and Éperney, always a useful watering-hole on my regular drives to the south of France.

Having had a break in the café there, I'd moved the car into the petrol station to refuel, ready for the next leg of the journey. It was there that I saw her, Jacqueline she was called, standing beside the car in front of me, struggling with the fuel cap. Noticing my number plate she asked, in her broken English, if I could help. In my broken French I said, "Of course," without hesitation. What male wouldn't have? Inept as I normally am at anything mechanical, the sight of perfection standing there brought out the rescue service mechanic within me.

Fortunately, all that was needed to resolve the problem was a little brute force, the usual male response in such matters anyway and the limit of my ability as regards the internal combustion engine.

Jacqueline was in her mid-twenties I'd guessed, the same as me but that was where the similarities ended. Where I was pale looking and average everything Jacqueline was tall and tanned, sun dressed and summer sandled, her hair the gold of that day with eyes that held the shades of the Mediterranean within them. The glow from her smile melted the tarmac from under my feet. With just the one look I fell completely under her spell.

She thanked me for my help. I said it was no problem, glad to have been of service and we went our separate ways, Jacqueline whizzing off in her silver-chic sports number, a car as sleek and as smart as herself, me trundling on behind in my nondescript piece of functionality. I was heading as far as Dijon, a rough halfway point where habit prescribed that I always made my stopover for the night.

Pulling into the hotel car park later I noticed Jacqueline's car, already parked. I put mine close by and walked into the lobby, looking around on the off-chance of seeing her. She'd checked in and was standing, waiting by the lift. She saw me looking and

I raised my hand to give a little wave in her direction. Jacqueline smiled and walked straight over to me. She thanked me again for helping earlier, which set us off on a conversation there in the hotel lobby as lifts came and went, people having to walk around us as if we were some sort of traffic island. It appeared that this hotel was a stopover for Jacqueline too, on her way to Nice though why she was heading there she didn't say and, being polite, I didn't ask.

I don't know why, it was certainly out of character for me, but as the conversation continued I asked her, an almost complete stranger, if she'd like to join me later for a drink. "Oui. Merci." Her response so quick she'd reverted to her native French.

And that, I guess, was the beginning of it all and the end of me.

It was all quite innocent to begin with, never intended it to be anything else. A drink in the bar, a little conversation to pass the evening, nothing more, but it soon became clear we were comfortable together, very comfortable, sitting there chatting in our mix of broken languages. After a couple of glasses I asked if she'd care to join me for dinner. Again there was no hesitation on her part and so I took her lightly by the elbow, guiding her to the restaurant.

Faces turned our way as we walked in though I'm sure it

was the woman at my side who was the point of attention, not the nondescript in the tee-shirt and blue jeans although, in my defence, I had added a jacket to my more usual ensemble, out of respect to my companion. Maybe it was the contrast between us that caused attention, I don't know. Either way, I didn't mind the varied looks, quite the opposite in fact. I was elated just to be seen with her, someone I'd have normally thought of as being well outside my sphere.

The evening passed in an enchantment. Tucked away in a far corner, we talked quietly together, heads close, almost conspiratorial, oblivious of the other diners. Our hands grazed each other's frequently. Jacqueline's eyes smiled incessantly. She never seemed to take them from me for a moment nor I, mine from her. It was a heady evening, intoxicating, bewitching.

By chance, our rooms were on the same floor. I walked her to her door. We stood, neither of us wanting nor able to move apart, magnetised in our positions. I'd meant merely to kiss her goodnight, formally, but as our lips brushed, touched, kissed I felt a tingle I'd never felt before with a woman. If there is such a thing as love at first sight then this was it. I'd never loved a woman as I did this one and knew instinctively I'd never love another.

As we stood there, in the hallway, I held her close, she held me tight. There was no way either was letting the other go which, of course, made it a little tricky to open the bedroom door! But open it we did and tumbled in, locked together as we were.

Lying there later in that afterglow with Jacqueline sleeping softly snuggled tight in my arm, I decided there and then that I'd request a transfer from London to the French office. I could work as easily from either. Rapidly planning myself a revised future, I slipped into my own sweet sleep, dreaming of a life in Provence with that woman.

Next morning came and, without warning, the world had changed. Overnight the poles, it seemed, had been reversed. Breakfast was the complete antithesis to the previous night's dinner, heavy where that had been light. Where she'd been ebullient Jacqueline was now quiet, remote. She barely spoke, certainly little more than words of one syllable. Even when I tried engaging her in conversation Jacqueline's responses were always brief, truncated, to the point.

We paid our respective bills and checked out, walking together to the car park with barely a word spoken. Time was slipping past. I'd originally intended to talk of the future over breakfast, but the frosty reception I'd had there made me wait until the point of leaving.

Jacqueline put her suitcase in the boot of her car and closed the lid. This was the last moment left. I moved to put my arms around her, give her a goodbye kiss, ask about any possible future, but she stepped back as if I had the plague. "Don't touch me," she said, adding a "Please," in softer tones.

Words abandoned me for the moment. The best I could answer was a mumbled, "What's wrong? Last night? This morning?" struggling to form a coherent sentence.

Reading the perplexity in my face she said, "I've fallen in love with you."

"So? Where's the problem in that?" Not understanding, now totally confused.

"I'm afraid that if I were to hold you again I'd never be able to let you go."

"If that's all, then don't let me go. It's quite simple."

"It's not 'quite simple', far from it," she said, "and I do have to let you go. I've no choice." With that, she took a further step back, her eyes falling to her shoes which seemed to hold a sudden fascination for her.

A single tear ran down her cheek as she turned on her heel and climbed into her car, driving out of the car park and out of my life just as smoothly as she'd driven into them.

The Lord of Lobsters
By Barbara Gibbons-Roscoe

I crawl out of my coral cave sifting the sea for my next prey. So many scents held in the ocean's bubbles. I float on a warm current until I find the one I must have next.

Curly clam resting on the bottom – that is my destination. Single existence is charmed.

Here is the man. He looks a little sad and not very fresh. Still, I must live. I thank the Lord of Clams before I eat. I remain a noble soul till the end, of course. I find interaction with my food too distasteful even to examine it.

Now it is time – to rest among the stones, time to burrow in the mud, time to sway on ocean's currents.

Fast rising to the round heat's kingdom, this cannot be good. Large tentacles suck at my sides. There is no swaying here, no sacred mud, no dreamy floating!

Such noise and preparations surround my cave. It is become of nets and lines – small and hard, crushing, hushing, sluicing, rushing, through and round. The eyes are large, the face is flat. How distasteful to be showing his teeth, there does not appear to be any civility here.

I try to breathe but the water is very thin. I find myself among the caves of my peers. This is extraordinary. I cannot keep my proper distance, I must withdraw inside. Within the shell is my space and my calm.

Moving again, I float once more – sweet buoyancy. But there is only a green horizon. No faraway sandy shore, no coral caves and shimmering seas. Instead there are more flat faces and repulsive teeth. Why has no-one told them teeth should be within, carefully sheltered away from another's gaze? They must be uncultured and unlearned to show their teeth.

Noise. Movement within movement I seem to fly, yet my horizon is still. This must be an arrival, the sky is red, although now surely it should be indigo?

Am I to be handled to sit among my brothers? Close quarters bring seaweed soothings and gritty landings. I swim again but face the glassy clarity of four walls. Once more the flat faces peer into my space. I am chosen and lifted into the thin water. Metallic circumference and rising steam. I see my death. I pray that flat face remembers to thank the Lord of Lobsters.

This short story was inspired by the following information: A lobster does have teeth – but they are not in its mouth, they are in its stomach. The food is chewed in the stomach between what look like three molars. Lobsters live a solitary life.

A Tale of Despair
By Eric Bulmer

The alarm went off, like a continuous explosion. They must have tripped some concealed switch; something which, in spite of all their meticulous planning, they had overlooked. Mind-numbing in its intensity the noise ricocheted from wall to wall of the cavernous subterranean power station.

For perhaps a second Woodham stood paralysed before his training took over. It was too late now, however. He knew that. Even if he could have stopped the alarm it would do no good. Soon, very soon, they would be here, swarming like so many infuriated soldier ants, those stocky, seemingly identical men he knew so well from the not-so-distant past, cradling their squat assault rifles – the ones that spewed out dum-dum bullets at such a rate they were virtually extruding lead bar from their ugly snouts.

"Don't freeze!" they'd screamed at him often enough in the training camp. "Whatever you do. Move! Anywhere! Freeze and you're dead!"

His companion on the steel catwalk was still staring wild-eyed at him as Woodham dived headlong into the impenetrable darkness. He hit the concrete twenty feet below with such force that bones snapped like over-dry firewood and soft, flabby, vital organs disintegrated. There was no pain. That, he knew, would come soon enough.

Raw terror held him face-down. Fear he'd known before in varying degrees, but this was a different breed, more extreme, more sapping than anything he'd ever experienced; this was fear of the known.

Silence hit him like a blow as the siren cut; a silence almost immediately shattered by the splintering of doors as they were kicked in. Then the clatter of those dreaded boots bringing back such horrific memories and a brief, barked command in that hated tongue. He remembered with a shudder how once, browsing a dictionary of their language, he'd found that they had no equivalent for the words 'pity' or 'compassion'.

He flinched and his broken teeth rattled together uncontrollably as the first wild shots splattered against the wall and pipework above him. His fingers clawed at the blood-stained concrete as his bowels and bladder involuntarily emptied themselves.

A longer burst of firing and a scream cut short a brief silence and then he was knocked almost unconscious by a weight crashing onto him. It was Clappison, or what was left of him, dead before his torn body spread itself messily over Woodham. At the camp everybody had pitied Clappison but now he was the one to be envied. He was dead and out of it.

Woodham felt a pleasing warmth on his face; it was the last few spurts of his friend's blood before it quickly congealed in the sub-zero temperature.

Why, oh why had he volunteered again? Was it for her? A need for revenge for what they had done to her? For some purpose in an empty life? Now he would never know.

It was useless and he knew it. Everything was lost, nothing salvageable. The whole mission a failure; all those long exhausting months of training were just so much wasted time. There was no escape and not the remotest chance of rescue; they'd been told that. They would be disowned and damned, an embarrassment.

He didn't try to move; there was nowhere to go. All the exits would be blocked by now. Even if by some miracle he had got outside the cold and the half-starved dogs would very quickly have finished him off.

A sudden thought flared into his mind and just as

quickly extinguished itself. What if he pleaded with them, told them everything, gave them all the names he knew, the passwords, the ciphers? Maybe then they would let him live even if it was a living death in one of their camps. But he knew this was absurd, they could extract all the information they needed so easily without any concessions. Passivity was the only way. Passivity and co-operation. They would be here any second now. And then. . .

And then he remembered it. The tiny box in his pocket, and in the box, the pill. They'd all laughed when the pills were handed out, all that is but Woodham. None of them had ever admitted that they could never use it. While there was life there was hope, they'd said. He knew better, he was the one who had suggested their issue. Now he was the only survivor. He almost smiled, so there was an escape route after all. It would be so easy, such a simple way to slip out of this existence, this infinite misery. Whatever followed couldn't be as bad as what was surely waiting if he didn't take this one chance of release.

It was an easy decision for him to take but not as easy to execute. Execute! There was an appropriate word, again he nearly smiled. Under the circumstances friends would have recognised the sense of humour.

He had to move fast, had to get the pill before they

got him. Clappison's corpse was heavy across the pocket and the pain at last struck as he struggled from under the already-rigoring body. Was it delirium or did his friend seem reluctant to release him, clutching at him in one last terrified embrace?

Clear of the encumbrance he could feel the box through the material of the pocket. His rapidly-numbing fingers tried to find the opening. "Please God let it be unbuttoned." It was and he grasped the longed-for box.

Above him he heard the echoing brutal commands as they searched the hall. A torch beam slashed down from the catwalk onto the two bodies. More shouts but now with an edge of cruel excitement to them. He knew enough of their tongue to gather that they wanted him alive if he was so. They would terminate him when and if it suited them.

The light moved away and he brought the box up to his mouth. In spite of the penetrating cold, sweat broke out on his forehead with the sudden awful realisation of what he was about to do.

This was it then, the end. A pitiful finish to a futile existence. His life had been as meaningful as that of a gnat.

He wept silently for the broken hulk that had once known the sun, the sky and her, wept for himself for there was no-one left to cry for him. Not since her.

The thin plastic of the box splintered between the wreckage of his teeth. The tip of his tongue felt the smooth roundness of the pill. All he had to do now was to manoeuvre it back and then, bite.

A ladder dropped over the safety rail; it smashed onto his legs and one of the men laughed. He saw the first one swing onto the ladder and start down while the others unnecessarily covered him with their rifles. As if he was going anywhere! Some remnants of a half-forgotten faith came back to him – fire and brimstone, whatever that was – haloes and harps, whatever they were. He would have prayed if he'd known how.

He bit hard on the sugar-coated pill as a boot kicked in the just-mended ribs. They had been told it would be painless and instant. "You won't feel a thing, it'll be just like going to sleep on a warm afternoon." They were wrong. Even his 'friends' had ultimately betrayed him.

The pain went off the scale of his experience. The hacking boots seemed almost a relief in comparison as his body arched and burnt, limbs flailing wildly. Spasmed muscles contorted his features into a gargoyle's mask. For the few wracked seconds left to him even the black-uniformed enemy stood back in awe. Then all senses – hearing, sight and mercifully pain – faded away to be replaced by a blackness more profound than the deepest night.

A light, painful in its intensity, burnt into his retina, surely blinding him. He tried to close his eyelids but some mechanism held them open.

His arms were strapped immovably to the arms of a chair. Someone came between him and the light and he looked longingly for her but it was the guard he saw drawing back a clenched fist. The interrogation he knew would last for eternity, began.

Search for an Ice Cream
By Mel Eldridge

The beach beyond the cliff-fall stood autumnal and deserted at the end of an overcast cool day. Tired, deflated and alone I pitched my tent on the top of the shingle bank beyond the wet stain of the high-water mark. Heavy grey clouds gave way to late sunshine that set in a pink blaze behind distant white cloud ribbons.

Dr Mac had given me a few weeks. He said my body had had enough of the drugs and alcohol, and he advised me to make final arrangements.

From my tent I watched the sunset. My father had brought me here for my ninth birthday. Twenty years ago, a memory of him and an ice cream. A sense of belonging, of love and the thought that the next day would be the same. They rarely are, but I hoped, and it wasn't. He disappeared without a goodbye.

On the beach, alone in my tent, I heard footsteps

accompanied by singing. I put my head out of the tent and had my first view of Claire. Late twenties with dirty brown boots, ripped blue jeans and green shirt and jersey. Her dark hair full of sand had been put in a ponytail which showed off her grimy young face. She had a bloodless gash above her right eye. She stopped singing, put her head on one side to study me. She noticed my old black kettle on the burner and asked if we could share, then pitched her tent next to mine.

We talked about our lives. We were kindred spirits that drifted here and there as our whims and fancies guided us. She'd run away from an abusive stepfather in Newcastle to London. She soon realised how dangerous it could be for a girl on her own with nowhere to stay once her money ran out, so she headed for the coast. We were both the flotsam and jetsam of life with our hopes and dreams crushed.

In truth, Claire didn't seem quite normal. Each day her skin became more pallid and her speech began to slur. I noticed the same had begun to happen to me but paid it no heed.

On the third morning, she was nowhere to be seen. Her belongings and the tent were in place. She had disappeared in the night. I waited for her. I had nowhere to be and I liked her. We understood each other. Later a walker appeared on the beach with a large black dog. He discarded a newspaper in a nearby waste bin. I called out, but he ignored me, oblivious to my existence but the dog barked several times in my direction.

A full moon came up on a golden night. It moved across the sky to cast a beam of light over the calm sea. From my tent, I watched it shine directly at me. A black shadow walked along the beam towards the shore. I sat transfixed because of what I could not believe. But there in front of me, Claire walked on the beam towards the shore. The spring tide had pushed up the beach to its furthest point. Claire stood as far as the beam would allow. She beckoned, both arms extended. Her hands urged me towards her. I watched in disbelief at this trick of the light, or perhaps a nightmare. I didn't know what to do, so I ignored her and closed the tent flaps. Typical of me. In truth a radio news item had spooked me. A boy and a girl both about Claire's age, had gone missing, believed buried under the nearby cliff fall.

The next night the same full moon, the same beam of light and there Claire stood. I could have ignored it again but I had tried that and Claire had returned. I felt drawn to her and in a trance moved forwards. My footsteps crunched on the pebbles and I stopped at the high-water mark. One more step and I would be on the beam of light. She hovered and shimmered and sang the song I'd heard the first time we met. She beckoned me with long sweeps of her arms. I didn't know whether I was dead or alive, but she seemed to offer a chance to belong, of love maybe. I sat on the shingle, removed my boots and socks then took my first step onto the beam of light. Claire urged me forward then turned and I followed. The opportunity to taste that childhood ice cream beckoned.

With Suburbia Slipping Past
By Chris Milner

It happens a lot, actually.

She grabs my wrist, pulls towards me, her face alight, hugs me hard, all the while breathlessly squealing to her friend, "Oh, it is you! Lizzie, look, look, it's Jenson. Jenson! Oh, wow!"

It's always women of a certain age, people like Lizzie and her friend. They feel they know me, feel I bring back a bit of their youth. Sometimes, they'll tell me how they saw Westwipe in Aberdeen or in Barnsley or Cardiff, way back in the day, and how fabulous it was and how sorry they are and all that.

But what can I do? I reckon it's much the best to let people believe what they want to believe – be considerate, let them dream, don't stamp on their memories – and always, always, leave them smiling.

So I turn to Dens and give her my favourite 'Patient

Suffering' face. Then I enjoy the embrace, thank Lizzie and friend for their love, wish them well and wave goodbye like the star they think I am.

Dens is cool with it all. She's new but she's alright.

Later, when we're on the train – when I'm comfortable no-one else is trying to catch a sneaky look at me, or whispering to their friends, or pointing – I tell Dens my great idea.

"I've had this great idea for a story, Dens. A real blockbuster."

"Oh, yes?"

"Yeah. It's about an upper-class twit who's got a bunch of mates who all get married one by one, leaving just him, and in the end he dies. Five weddings and a Funeral. What do you think?"

"It's been done."

"No! Honestly?"

"Yup. Big success. Pity you didn't think of it before."

We fall silent and I concentrate on the view, watching all suburbia slipping past the carriage window. Everywhere here looks the same – short, narrow gardens behind overgrown trees, wires fencing off the railway lines, running up to shabby little terraced houses, curtains all drawn, lights all off.

"No-one home, Dens."

"I guess not."

"Where are we going?"

"Wokingham. To see an old friend."

As the train slows and pulls lethargically into Virginia Water station, I take a hard look at the trees, their shadows and the glimpses between them to somewhere beyond. "This looks familiar, Dens. I think I've been here before."

"You have. You had a place here before you went to Afghanistan."

"I did? I don't remember going to Afghanistan."

"No pet. That's where everything changed and you. . ."

"Hey, Dens, I've had an idea for a great story."

"Oh, yes?" She has that smirk some carers will give you. "Is this where an ordinary upper-class twit has a bookshop in North London and this glamorous American film star comes in one day and falls for his simple upper-class charms?"

"No! That's amazing! You read my mind. How did you. . ."

"Just a hunch. You've told it to me before."

"Oh, bugger!" What else is there to say? "Bugger, bugger, bugger!"

The train is one of those rattling toytown trains. They don't go fast, probably can't. They look quite new, probably are. The seats are too small, probably so they can pack in the punters.

Maybe they should make it okay to sit on other

commuters' laps once all the seats are taken. It could revolutionise rail travel, double passenger numbers overnight.

I think of telling Dens about my idea but I'm not sure I want her telling me again that it's already been thought of, that they're already doing it all over the country. Anyway we're pulling into another station and Dens is getting the bag down, a sure sign it's time to get off.

"This is Wokingham."

"No shit," I reply, just to show her I'm not so stupid.

We have to wait while the train guard sets up the little steel bridge to let my wheelchair run onto the platform. He's one of those kind-but-brusque sorts and gives me a big smile. But not one that screams Westwipe fan, just a smile.

As we make our way down the platform, a large guy in a leather jacket comes out of the entrance and makes his way towards us, grinning wide. He's certainly recognised me.

"Hey, Jenson!" he calls from way off. This guy is huge and he's getting huger with every step.

I look at Dens and mutter, "Here we go again," and give her my 'Patient Suffering' face mixed with an improvised 'For Goodness Sake Look at the Size of this Guy' face. It's hard to pull them both off together, but I think I manage it.

He hugs me hard.

"Good to see you, Jenson! Looking good, my man!"

"Thanks," I say. "Very nice to meet you," staying as limp as I can in his giant embrace.

"It's Bobby, Jenson," says Dens. "Remember Bobby?"

I'm not sure where to start. Remembering Bobby, or wondering why Dens has now started thinking I'm Jenson too.

"Sure you remember, don't you buddy," says big guy. "Oh, we had some great times, didn't we? And some great tours. All except that last one of course."

He's suddenly stopped in his oversize tracks, looking distant. "Forces concerts. They never really warn you do they?"

But then he's hugging Dens and she's all flushed and beaming. That's a new one. Not so cool now, are you Dens.

"And those crowds, Jenson. You can't have forgotten that gig we did at the O2. Those girls, all those girls!"

He laughs aloud to encourage me so I look at him and smile.

Whoever these crazy people are, they're obviously in this together. I'll play along for now and slip away later. Like I say, best to let people believe what they want to believe. . . and always, always, leave them smiling.

Biographies

Girl in Shorts   **Yvonne Ayres**

After a varied career working mostly in fashion, on retirement I decided to develop my lifelong love of writing. I now pen articles for my local parish magazine and have had a few short stories published in women's magazines. I live in Stansted Mountfitchet with my husband and have two children and one grandson.

The Game   **Celia Berggreen**

I retired from teaching a few years ago and joined The Creative Writing Programme in Brighton. After three years I finished my debut novel, and am now working on novel two. I live in Mid Sussex with my Danish husband, and love spending time with any of my eight grandchildren.

Cedar Heights   **Clive Boothman**

Enjoying living in Kendal for the outdoor opportunities it presents – cycling and walking being my main fresh air hobbies, but also enjoy reading, writing and yoga. My main writing to date has been poetry, but my success as a runner up points me in another possible direction.

A Tale of Despair   **Eric Bulmer**
I am a Northerner living for three years down South.
By trade I was a university zoology technician. About
ten months ago I joined a writing group and enjoy
correcting, modifying and polishing my writing as much
as the writing.

Mick Jagger and Mum   **Mary Charnley**
Mary lives in Cornwall with her husband and dog. She
has been writing for many years and recently gained an
MA in Creative Writing from the University of Lancaster.
She likes to write stories around the challenges and
pleasures of old age. Her first novel *Resurrecting Alice* was
published recently.

The Old Storyteller   **Robert Crockett**
In my working life I was a Deputy Headteacher at a school
for children with learning difficulties. In my childhood
I was brought up with a love of books and the joy of
reading, especially history and historical fiction. Apart
from writing I enjoy singing and following sport.

The Fancy Dress Party   **Maisie Dance**

I was secretary of the Croydon Writers for 22 years. My book *Two Acres of Love* was published by Honeywood Museum in Carshalton, Surrey four years ago and it is still sold in their shop. I have had poetry published as well as articles and short stories over the years.

The Seagull   **Michael Downes**

I was born and raised in Northern Ireland. I came to Australia as a twenty year old in 1971. I have written over seventy short stories, six novellas, a three-act play and four novels. My fourth novel, a drama, deals with my adventures in a remote mining town in Queensland.

Stella's a Star   **Jean Duggleby**

I am a retired primary teacher and worked with deaf children. I started writing short stories after attending a creative writing course. I live in east London with my partner and have a married daughter and two grandchildren in New Zealand. I like walking, gardening, reading, travel and teach circle dancing.

Search for an Ice Cream   **Mel Eldridge**
Mel grew up in Hastings, graduated university with a Law Degree and worked in Local Government. He writes adult and children's fiction, short stories and flash. Local writing groups helped him improve as a writer. With various writing projects on the go he would like more time!

Kiteflying on Aranmore   **Tina Enlander**
Tina Enlander has been married to Ian for over 35 years and is the mother of three adult children. Having recently retired from a career as a Social Worker and Art Therapist she is now enjoying a return to creativity both as an artist and as a writer.

The Lord of Lobsters   **Barbara Gibbons-Roscoe**
Barbara has had a varied career including book editing, environmental research, and running a B&B. She began writing with contributions to the school newspaper. She has published three non-fiction books and successfully completed an Open University course in Creative Writing. Barbara is working towards her first extended fictional manuscript.

Such Stuff as Dreams are Made of   **Janet Hender**
Originally from London, my husband and I have lived in rural Staffordshire for many years. I belong to a small writing group meeting periodically to read aloud and discuss each other's short stories. I find the process of paring down a short story to its true essence very satisfying.

Matthew on Thursdays   **Rita Houghton**
I have always loved books. Daphne du Maurier inspired me, after reading Rebecca, to write a short story with a surprise ending. To my surprise it was accepted and published. After that the hard work and a lot of homework followed. I hope to continue writing stories a reader enjoys.

Turn Back the Clock   **Janet Killeen**
Yorkshire-born Janet Killeen taught English for 37 years before retirement opened up opportunities to write short stories, exploring choice, time and the significance of landscape. In 2017 she published her first novel, *After the Flood*, set in the Somerset Levels in 2014, and is currently working on a sequel.

A Winter's Tale   **Peter Lewis**
I'm married with three daughters and live in Wigan, Greater Manchester. I'm a retired teacher and my spare time is filled with being chair of school governors, holidaying in France and writing. I've self-published a novel *A Snow Fox in Normandy* and an anthology of short stories, *The Flying Coffin*.

Winter   **Lynn Loader**
I was born in Suffolk and after thirty years in Yorkshire I recently retired back to East Anglia. My working life was spent as a translator. I love books, animals and the outdoors, spend an inordinate amount of time bird-watching, and draw my inspiration from the natural world.

Each Day as it Comes   **Gwenda Major**
Gwenda lives in the Lake District. Her stories have featured in numerous publications, both print and digital. She has also written four novels and two novellas: her novella *Offcomers* won first prize in the NAWG Open Novella competition in December 2016. Gwenda has a website at www.gwendamajor.wordpress.com

Flames   **Lindsey Malin**
Lindsey Malin (nee Macfarlane) is long retired from her
work as a curator at the National Maritime Museum in
Greenwich where she wrote Marine Oils in 1992. She
now lives with her husband in South East London and
spends time painting and, more recently, writing.

The Dim Reaper   **John Maskey**
John Maskey was born and brought up in Newcastle.
He has worked as a journalist on local and national
newspapers. After living in Cheshire, Essex and London,
he returned to Northumberland with his wife and three
children. He has written a trilogy for teenagers and is
seeking a publisher.

As You Sow   **Jim McGuirk**
Jim McGuirk is a retired electronics engineer. He and
his partner Nel have been together for over 50 years and
have four children, three grandchildren and one great-
grandchild. He spends his leisure time writing and his first
book, *Short Short Stories for Busy Busy People*, is available
on Amazon.

With Suburbia Slipping Past **Chris Milner**
After years making software, writing manuals, creating small social enterprises, running charities, Chris has retired to Hexham, Northumberland, where he lives with his wife and enjoys journeys and playing Grandpa. He began telling stories by joining a writing group and revels in the big reveal.

Friendship **Valerie Nye**
I am married, with two children and three grandchildren. I was a teacher in secondary and further education, and also involved in assessments and the NVQ. I was always interested in writing and after retiring decided to try to develop this interest.

City Walk **Christopher Owen**
Christopher's stories have been published in magazines in the UK and US and long-listed for the V.S. Pritchett Short Story Prize 2018 and Dorset Fiction Award 2018. *An Honourable Man* won Final Chapters Competition 2014. His plays have been performed in the UK, Gulf States, Ireland, Australia and US. www.christopherowen.co.uk

Second Home   **Terry Parsons**
Brought up on the western edge of the New Forest, I have
been writing off and on (more off than on, I'm afraid) for
many years. With writing, as with other arts, persistence
seems almost as necessary as ability. Favourite authors
include Kingsley Amis, Waugh, Orwell, Hardy and
Wodehouse.

Midsummer Magic   **Linda Preston**
As a child I was probably one of the most frequent
borrowers at the village library. I wrote stories for fun.
English Literature at GCE put me off fiction for years.
At the age of 50 I rediscovered novels and the joy of
imagination. I'm catching up on the lost years.

A Brief Encounter   **Ian Riddle**
Ian began his first novel, *Midsummer Dreams*, only two
years ago. As a break from it he wrote a couple of short
stories which culminated in his first work, *Collected
Writings – Vol I*, published in 2018. *Vol II* is now ready for
publication. A novella is well on the way.

Falling into the Dark   **Linda Roberts**
I'm a retiree living in Guernsey with my partner Paul.
Writing is something I seriously took up on retiring. I've
always had a passion for it and enjoy writing short stories
and flash fiction, especially adding a twist to the end.

Marilyn's Letters   **Ann Taylor**
As a retired teacher from Surrey, I had never tried my hand
at writing until last year when I discovered how difficult,
creative and addictive it is. It's great to disappear inside
another character and make them do things I would never
dream of doing.

A Sound Journey   **Harriet Townsend**
Harriet Townsend trained at the Rose Bruford Drama
College and has taught, acted and directed in the West
Indies, Turkey, Greece and the UK. She now lives in
Saltaire World Heritage Site, West Yorkshire, where she
has written and directed numerous successful shows
and events based on its history.

The Girl by the Wall   **Jane Varley**
I spent most of my working life no further north than Oxfordshire. I moved to the glorious Peak District when I retired. Living here reunites me with the joys of childhood in Devon and Somerset. I have always 'tinkered' with writing. Now more leisure time encourages me to write more.

The Date   **Sandy Vaughan**
Having spent my working life as a lexicographer, proofreader and technical author, upon retiring I decided to try my hand at fiction. Writing stories has opened up a whole new world, one which is exciting, challenging, and has released previously unsuspected creativity. I live and write in rural Oxfordshire.

Parallel Lives   **David Watson**
David Watson was educated at the Beal Grammar School and subsequently had a career as a consulting engineer. David has lived his whole life in Essex and is a lifelong, keen, amateur artist. He also loves to write short stories and poetry and hopefully that elusive novel is getting closer.

All Sides of the Story **Anne Whitehead**

I live in Devon with my husband and am very much enjoying my retirement, which has freed up time to do things I like to do and also explore other interests. I've always loved reading and urban tramping around, both of which feed into my writing.

Going Somewhere **Beth Wildberry**

Beth Wildberry was born in London in 1936. Her childhood was spent in Kent, Sussex and Ontario, Canada. After raising her family of four she graduated with a degree in English Literature from Sussex University. She lives with her partner in West Sussex where she is a slave to the garden!

The Moth **Keith Windsor**

I am a retired engineer trying to do art and writing. Living by the South Downs, inspiration for the art bit is easy, the writing bit. . . Aargh! I have to dredge memories and incidents from life and then, well just hope!